The Curse of BRIARWOOD

THE CURSE OF BRIARWOOD

E.B. WHEELER

Rowan Ridge
Press

ISBN: 978-1-960033-19-2

First printing: July 2025

Published by Rowan Ridge Press, Utah

Cover design © Rowan Ridge Press

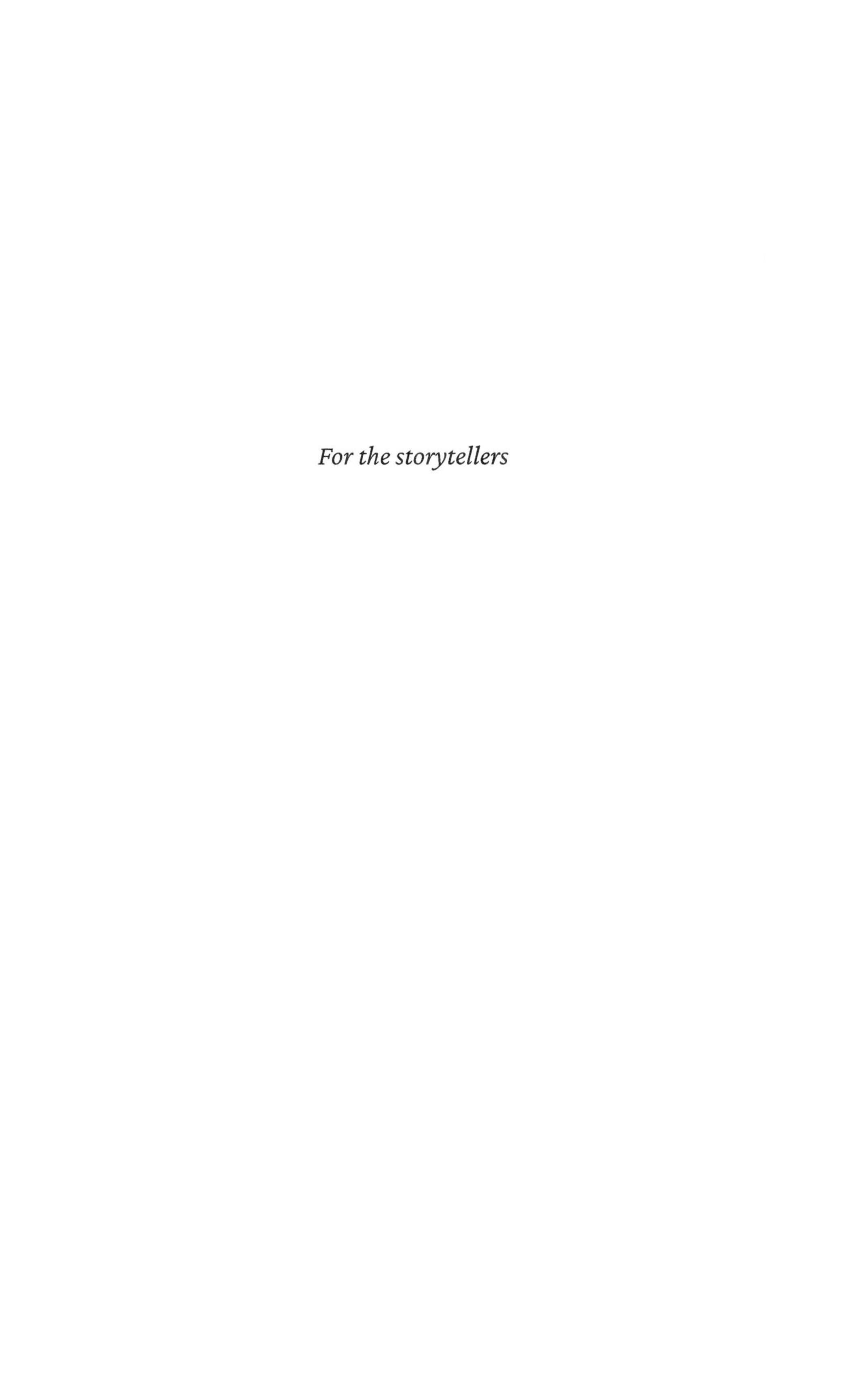

For the storytellers

CHAPTER 1

My brother's hired carriage hauled me toward Bath much as I imagined the tumbrel carted Paris ladies to the guillotine. Like those lost souls, I would never be returning home. The rumble of the wheels echoed in my ears like a murmur of voices. Impatient. Angry. Mocking. No matter how I huddled under my cloak, my hands were icy, and I could not escape those whispers, as if all of England gossiped about me.

It didn't help that my brother Julian and his new wife Frances *were* speaking of me.

I hadn't intended to eavesdrop. Dusk fell, and I grew weary of listening to Frances chatter about all the wealthy, well-connected men in Bath who were so old and senile they might marry almost anyone—perhaps even me! So, I shut my eyes and feigned sleep.

"I don't see why you're so quick to take Athena to Bath,"

my brother Julian grumbled to Frances. "It's expensive, and she's always been so efficient at home."

I *had* been efficient at home. Efficient. Useful. Appreciated. I had even allowed myself a hazy daydream that it might someday lead to being loved. An ache burrowed into my chest. What a fanciful story to keep kindled in the secret hearth of my imagination. Frances had thrown reality over it like icy water.

"We can afford it, thanks to me," Frances said primly. "And it's past time for poor Athena to be out in the world."

Yes, Frances wanted to be rid of me, and Bath was her best gamble. Frances was thinking of doddering men haunting the ballrooms and salons—a connection to anchor her social position more securely. I was thinking of gouty old ladies in the pump room seeking a lady's companion. Bath also had girls' schools and young families in need of governesses, but after my family's scandal, no Mama would want me around her children. I could handle difficult elderly ladies and their demands, though. They could never be worse than Frances.

"She's never expressed much interest in being out in society," Julian said, his voice almost lost beneath the steady beat of the horses' hooves.

Frances sniffed. "Well, it isn't fair to keep her where she will always be in my shadow. It was one of the conditions of our marriage, after all, that we would find a more suitable situation for your sister."

I had not been aware of that. I drew my shoulders in as if I could disappear entirely into the dim corner of the carriage. I was not wanted anywhere. My eyes stung, but I kept them squeezed shut. Crying wasn't practical. It would do nothing for me. What else had I expected when Julian married? No wife wanted to share her household with another lady, watching the servants second guess her and look to someone else for instruction. I had been *too* efficient.

Julian cleared his throat. "But after my father—"

"Hush," Frances snapped. "Leave that in the past. After all, I was still willing to marry you. She's not a lost cause—not with *my* help. Your father kept her too much at home, but I will manage everything now."

My brother was right, though. No one would marry me after our father's disgrace. Scandal ran in families, or at least so everyone believed. I had long known that I was not destined for romance—I was the practical girl in the background who people relied on but did not admire. If I could have married someone who wasn't a beast, who valued my usefulness and let me have my own little garden as a refuge...

The knot in my stomach tightened, souring my mouth.

That had been an empty dream even before the scandal. No, my best hope was a position as a companion to some cantankerous old lady who cared more for an attentive assistant than what the gossips said.

I peeked with one eye just long enough to see the dark woods of the hills surrounding Bath faintly illuminated by the carriage lantern. The shadows beyond stretched like the fingers of an angry phantom, and ghostly figures wavered among the trees. I shivered and squeezed my eyes shut again, wishing I could truly sleep until we arrived at our lodgings. I had never been to Bath, or much of anywhere. Father had gone alone to his haunts in London. The lack of connection to Father was one of Bath's advantages, along with smaller crowds and less competition.

"Whoa!" the coachman cried.

The carriage jerked, nearly tossing me from my seat. I gasped and flung my hand out to brace myself against the cracked leather padding the carriage wall, expecting the vehicle to tumble into a ditch.

"What the devil—" Julian exclaimed.

"Stand and deliver!" came a male voice outside the carriage.

"Are we being robbed?" my brother demanded.

The carriage door beside Julian swung open to reveal a long, hideous face with pale skin and a twisted smile. I drew a sharp breath to scream for help against the ghoul. No, not ghoul: a man in a Carnival mask. I caught my breath, but my pulse continued to race—the masked man held a pistol.

"Of all the outrages!" Frances said. "How dare you hold us up?"

"Didn't you know, highwaymen are quite common along this stretch of road," the man replied, his voice muffled by the mask but laughter in his tone. "Never fear, though. I am one of the gallant variety of highwaymen who only wants your jewelry and will then let you pass on unmolested. Now, out of the carriage."

Frances gasped in outrage, and Julian seemed to have turned to stone.

"We had better do what he says." It was up to me to be sensible. Practical.

"You would say that," Frances grumbled. "It's not your money he's stealing."

I gritted my teeth, but Frances let Julian help her from the carriage.

When my brother forgot to offer me a hand, the highwayman did instead. I hesitated. I should have refused, but I was annoyed with Julian and Frances. I took the man's hand. His grip was firm but gentle as he helped me down with practiced ease, steadying me as I took a moment to adjust to ground that didn't sway beneath me. He wasn't just gallant; I suspected he was well-bred.

The highwayman glanced at his armed companion, who wore a grotesque, grinning mask and carried a blunderbuss. The henchman nodded in silent agreement of something.

"Be on your best behavior while I search your carriage," the highwayman warned us.

Julian and Frances fumed but dared not move while the henchman kept his blunderbuss on us. I stood in a beam of light from the carriage lamp, trying to conjure a bit of warmth against the chilly autumn night.

The highwayman poked his head into the carriage. "A hired vehicle. No secret compartment, then. Ah, here we are."

The highwayman pulled Frances's jewelry box from under the seat and set it on the stoop of the carriage. In full view, he rummaged through our valuables, studying each one and setting most aside. Even I flushed at the insult, and Frances was as hot as an oven next to me.

The man dug out one piece and shook his head. "Paste!"

"It is not!" Frances replied.

He laughed. "I'm not certain if you're trying to fool me or if someone else has fooled you, but I assure you, this is paste. Hmm. And this one is a family heirloom. Certainly worth more in sentiment than in the old jewels set in it. Ah, here we are. For your toll, I will take this fine necklace."

We all stared at him as he dumped Frances's things back into the box and pocketed a necklace with a large garnet.

"Those are *all* fine jewels!" Frances protested. "Only the best."

"Would you like me to steal more of them?" he asked, placing his hand on the box.

She shut her mouth and glared.

"Now, I will need the jewelry you have on your person as well."

His henchman shifted his grip on his blunderbuss.

My hands trembled—from fear, anger, or some compound of both—but I removed my glove. Then I hesitated, staring at the delicate gold ring etched with leaves and flowers I always wore on my smallest finger. It had belonged to my mother, who cherished beautiful things.

"Certainly you don't care for personal items of little value," I said, trying to sound reasonable instead of pitiful.

He studied me for a moment. "I am sorry, but everyone must pay their toll."

I glanced again at my mother's ring, then shut my eyes and wiggled it off. It would do me little good if I were dead. My skin felt wrong without the ring, like a part of me was missing. I ran my finger over the delicate circle once more, memorizing its feel, then dropped it in the highwayman's outstretched hand.

Frances harumphed and removed her rings as well.

"The gentleman, too," the highwayman said.

Julian gave a start and fumbled about his person. "I don't have much. Er, here is my watch fob."

It was true; we had sold absolutely everything after Father's death. I had only selfishly clung to the little gold ring, wishing for some beauty in my life, so perhaps this was a fitting punishment.

The masked man weighed the items in his hand, studying them as he had the other jewelry. I couldn't guess what he was looking for.

Something moved at the edge of my sight, and the henchman shouted a warning. The highwayman whirled, blocking the driver who had come up behind him with a cudgel. The highwayman knocked the hapless driver to the ground and turned his pistol between us and the man.

Frances screamed and swooned against Julian. Caught off guard, he nearly dropped her to the dirt road.

The highwayman turned to the driver. "Brave, but not very wise. Now I will need a hostage to help my retreat."

The highwayman glanced at us.

"You would not dare to touch me!" Frances shrieked.

"No, I think I would not like to," the highwayman said.

If I were not so angry with the highwayman, I might have chuckled. Frances keened louder. The henchman tensed. He might shoot us just to make Frances stop.

"Oh, I will go," I said.

I was, after all, the *efficient* one.

I approached the highwayman, stepping carefully to avoid the deep ruts in the road. "I do not know much of being a hostage. I suppose I must shield your escape."

"Indeed. For one with no experience in the role, you are

remarkably clear-headed." He leaned a little closer. "Aren't you frightened?"

I shrugged one shoulder. My hands still trembled a little, but I did not think the highwayman wanted to harm anyone.

"At least it frees me from the screaming for a moment," I whispered with a quick glance at Frances.

The highwayman chuckled. "True enough. Very well. You must only walk a little distance with me to ensure that no one else tries anything brave. Though, I think the bravest member of your party is here with me."

I looked to the hard-packed dirt road, not certain how to respond to that.

He backed away from the carriage and our driver, keeping his pistol handy but not pointing it at anyone in particular. Yes, this was a peculiar highwayman, well-mannered, selective about what he stole, and not wishing to shoot. I wondered what made him turn to highway robbery. But I asked nothing, just walked obediently between him and the carriage until he reached a horse hobbled in the shadows of the trees. His henchman followed, always keeping his blunderbuss on Julian, Frances, and the driver.

"That ought to do," the highwayman told me.

He swept a bow to me and held out his gloved hand. I hesitated and stared at his mask. I could just make out dark eyes behind the grotesque face. I placed my hand in his, not sure what to expect, but trusting that he wasn't about to abduct me. Why steal what no one else wanted to have?

He placed a kiss on the back of my hand and slipped my mother's ring back onto my finger. His touch was warm and surprisingly gentle. I stared at him in confusion. He placed

Frances's wedding ring in my palm, then swept off his hat and waved it to the carriage.

"Until we meet again, my friends."

Before Frances could summon a renewed burst of outrage, the highwayman and his henchman rode off into the shadows. I stared at my mother's ring and then where the highwayman had disappeared for a long moment before turning reluctantly to the carriage. When I thought of what lay before me, I almost wished he *had* carried me off.

What a silly girl I was. My little brush with adventure was over, and I should be grateful. I survived a highwayman unharmed. In fact, as I returned Frances's ring and climbed back into my corner in the carriage, I felt a sliver of hope that I might face my guillotine and come away with my head intact.

CHAPTER 2

Our lodgings in Bath overlooked Queen Square, and I watched the fashionable men and women parading past the tall houses of polished tan stone with the knot in my stomach growing tighter each day, until I could barely force myself to eat. What would Bath society make of us? Of me? No one came to call even after Frances delivered her calling cards to every acquaintance in the city. They only had to see the surname Ratliff to steer well away.

I would do all that was proper and required of me, of course, but I couldn't help missing my mother's garden and wishing I could be free of the house. The weak sunlight filtering through the windows felt cold, and the songs of birds were muffled by the constant rattle of carriages, barking of dogs, and calls of peddlers. If I sometimes found my gaze wandering from the muddle of Bath up to the wild, open hills around the city and wondering about highway-men, well, I hardly thought I could be blamed.

Frances, on the other hand, glanced up from her embroidery or bonnet-decorating from time to time to glare at the passersby beyond the glass panes. She then went back to work with savage efficiency, her brow knit in a thoughtful frown.

"Enough of this," she proclaimed after we had been in Bath almost a week. "We will attend the Assembly Ball tonight."

Julian grimaced. "Do you think that wise?"

"Leave all to me," Frances said with a self-assured smile. "I will drop a few words about our encounter with the highwayman, and we'll have the *beau-monde* eating from our hands."

I didn't dare point out that our meeting with the highwayman hardly made us less scandalous. The sooner Frances's match-making failed, the sooner I could escape into my plan of becoming a lady's companion. I would make the most of our time in Bath.

"Can we also see the Roman Baths?" I blurted instead before I could second-guess myself. "If we're going out anyway?"

"Hmm." Frances studied me. "I suppose that would be acceptable. It will give you something interesting and appropriate to talk about while you dance."

I gritted my teeth but didn't object to her evaluation of my conversational abilities.

She vanished for a couple of hours that afternoon but returned in plenty of time to ensure we were dressed to her satisfaction, placing extra ostrich feathers in my hair until I felt freakishly tall and plumed.

At least she did not fail in her promise to let us visit the ruins on our wall to the Upper Assembly Rooms.

A warm mist rose off the baths for which the city was named, chasing the evening chill from my skin. The rectangular pool lined with columns bubbled a murky green in the evening light, and I could almost imagine ghosts lingering on its edges. They would not be the intruders there, where they had remained with the ancient stones almost two thousand years. No, it was we who were just a passing moment in the long history of the place.

Making certain Frances was not watching, I slipped off my glove and rested my fingertips on the time-worn column, imagining all the things that must have passed before it.

Something white moved at the corner of my eye, but I was careful not to look directly. When I was young, I often thought I saw the ghost of a long-dead ancestress in the west corridor at night. My governess, Miss Davidson, had quickly disabused me of any such fanciful notions, though.

An imagination is unbecoming in a young lady. You have no use for such tales.

So, I had dutifully ignored the poor lady in her long, pale gown. Over time, she vanished from my sight.

"The smell." Frances waved her fan before her nose. "Like sulfur! And this dampness will do no good for our hair. Oh, but don't mention any of that when you dance tonight, Athena. Come, you've both had your peek; we must be going."

I turned obediently. Julian lingered just a moment, and we shared a look of regret, but then we trailed after Frances like goslings after their mother. She hailed men carrying sedan chairs to bear us through the fashionable districts to the Upper Assembly Rooms.

The Assembly Rooms were fairly short and made of the same tan stone as the rest of the city. Not too intimidating, though the high windows prevented me from seeing the size of the crowd inside. The columns at the entrance gave the building a classical air. Our new gowns with their pale colors, high waists, and loose skirts were supposed to harken back to classical times, too, and I wondered if that pleased the ghosts of the place.

A crowd of men in elaborate cravats and women in draping gowns streamed past us and into the building. I'd never seen so many people at once in my life, and I shrank from their notice, my mouth too dry even for the most banal polite conversation. This was to be my Bath debut. Thank heavens Frances had not tried our luck in London! I would have been completely lost at Almack's—though with my family's scandal, I needn't have feared ever being admitted to that illustrious society.

Frances guided us inside and to the dance hall. The song of violins poured from the musician's balcony overhead, and people both dancing and observing formed a crush in the long, rectangular room. The heat and humidity washed over me, reminding me of the Roman pool after all. It was only September and the Bath Season hadn't begun in earnest. But birds...worms... We were certainly early birds, and I was supposed to be grateful if even a worm of a man would condescend to accept me and my scandal and my pitiable dowry.

No. I would be shunned, and Frances would see that this

was a terrible idea. I would become some lady's companion, and we could all have some peace. I only had to endure and avoid any unpleasant attention.

Heads turned as we entered the room, and whispers fled around the crowd, swift as a greyhound. I tightened my grip on my fan, resisting the urge to hide my face behind it.

"I'll go to the card rooms, then," Julian muttered.

"You will not!" Frances breathed. "Think what people will say!"

Yes, our father's troubles had started at the card tables.

"Circulate among the men, instead," Frances whispered. She took my arm. "We only need a few minutes, and I'll have Athena taken care of."

I wanted to avoid the gossip wafting through the rooms like the stink of a sewer on a hot day, but Frances's strategic rumormongering worked its desired effect. I could see the debate her acquaintances faced: no one wanted to be associated with Father's scandal, but everyone wanted to hear about the robbery, for highwaymen were the favorite villains of the *beau-monde*. Slowly, those who avoided our respectable address in Queen Square made their way over to greet Frances on the neutral ground of the ballroom.

She was happy to oblige them with a vastly exaggerated account of our adventure, speaking loudly enough to be heard over the violins playing their cotillion. I was happy to shuffle aside and stay out of their notice.

"And then, the scoundrel returned my ring and kissed my knuckles!" Frances finished, displaying her gloved hand for all to admire.

Her little audience gasped and tittered.

I remained outside her circle and kept my gaze on my fan. It would be unwise—silly—to point out it was my hand he had kissed. What did it matter? But Frances had not been close enough to see the laughter in the highwayman's dark eyes.

To my surprise, the Master of Ceremonies approached me with a young man in tow. That could only mean the young man wished to dance with me. I stood even straighter, resisting the urge to look over my shoulder and make certain he wasn't aiming for someone else. A bead of sweat tickled between my shoulder blades. The young man had to be properly introduced to me in order for us to dance or even speak. He would hear my shameful family name before he could know anything else about me.

"Athena Ratliff," I whispered to the Master of Ceremonies when he asked to know me.

Well-bred as he was, he hesitated momentarily at the name. A memorable one. My skin flushed. If only I was Jane Smith and easily forgotten.

"Miss Athena Ratliff, may I present Mister John Cunningham," The Master of Ceremonies said quickly. He departed, his duty complete.

Mr. Cunningham stiffened slightly at my name. I raised my eyes to his, waiting for the inevitable.

He swallowed and looked over his shoulder as if wishing to call the Master of Ceremonies back for rescue. "Miss Ratliff," he said. "Forgive the intrusion. I thought you were… someone else…a sister of a school friend."

I took pity on him. "I'm sorry to have disappointed you, Mr. Cunningham. But I think perhaps a friend is summoning you to the card room?"

"Yes, thank you!" He bowed and nearly scampered to the card room and the imaginary friend.

I sighed. The heat and noise of the room bore down on me, making my head ache, and I wished I could scamper away as well.

"I would have made him dance with me," muttered an elderly lady sitting in one of the chairs along the wall behind me.

I started and turned to her. I should have ignored the woman since we weren't acquainted, but there was a glitter in her eye that intrigued me. This seemed just the sort of unconventional gray-haired matron who might look to someone like me as a hired companion.

"It would not have been practical," I said. "If I spent my energy on everyone who slighted me, I would have little left for anything else. No, he is not worth the time a dance would take."

She chuckled. "Good girl. Yes, I heard your name. Unfortunate, but gossip is a hot flame that burns itself out quickly, at least in a place like Bath. Already tongues are wagging about the comte and his daughter over there."

She gestured with the knob of her ebony cane to a regal man in a powdered wig and a petite young lady hovering in his shadow.

"The Comte de Carriere and Mademoiselle de Carriere. Recently escaped from France," the woman said.

My mouth formed an "o," and I tried not to gawk.

"Indeed, they are a source of much interest." She sounded amused, and definitely unimpressed. "And then, there is Lord Neale."

With her eyes, she indicated a man standing on the far side of the room. The crowd parted around him like the Red Sea fleeing Moses. He watched them all with a bored smirk, the sleeve of his somber suit marked by a mourning band, his brown hair unpowdered, his dark eyes arresting.

"And who is he?" I whispered.

"Someone whose name will always be more tainted than yours. Some say he killed his sister last year. A charming girl whom everyone loved. They say he was jealous of her popularity and wanted to control her—and now his household is cursed for his sins."

Murder? Curses? I inhaled sharply, and I would swear that Lord Neale looked in my direction.

I turned quickly to my informant. "Surely none of that can be true!"

She smiled sadly. "Does that matter if everyone else has decided it is?"

I risked a glance back at Lord Neale and found him watching me. My face warmed, and I flicked my fan open with a snap to cool myself and hide my interest.

"I would think it does matter," I whispered. "At least to his sister."

The elderly lady nodded. "I agree. We have to take our stories back from those who would smear our names."

I looked sharply at this lady, realizing that I did not know who she was, and that no one else was speaking to her. Was she a fellow outcast?

Before I could find a polite way to ask more about her, I saw Frances summoning me.

"Excuse me," I said.

Frances had drifted farther up the hall, so I had to wend my way through the streams of people.

"Thief!" one lady muttered to another as I passed.

They scooted aside so that even the hems of their gowns would not brush mine.

My breath caught as if I'd been shoved. My slippers seemed to stick on the polished wood floor, and I almost whirled to the ladies. I was not my father. I was not to blame. But a lady did not make a scene. I kept my head down and walked on.

Frances watched me with narrow eyes. "Who was that elderly lady you were speaking to?"

"An...acquaintance." I avoided looking back at the woman.

"Unless she knows some eligible gentlemen, you should not waste your time. We must have you dancing. My influence ought to help you find a partner."

She glanced around as if the desired gentlemen would materialize, but she could not force young men to speak to me.

"Do not frown," she said, keeping her tone low. "How can I help you if you will not be pleasant?"

I forced myself to wear a polite smile the entire time as eyes darted my way and ladies whispered behind their fans.

I did not dance that night.

When Julian rejoined us at the end of the evening, he looked thoughtful. Almost sad.

"You did not sneak off to the card room, I hope." Frances did not look at him, adjusting the fingers of one glove as she spoke.

Julian winced. "I did not."

But something troubled him. He cast almost nervous glances at me as we worked our way outside the building. I wondered what he had overheard about me. My chest tightened at the thought. But it was for the best that Julian heard it. He would understand why I would take a position as a lady's companion and be grateful for it.

Sedan chairs carried us back to our lodgings. I wondered if the brawny men carrying our chairs also knew the name Ratliffe and despised it.

Once home, Frances patted me on the shoulder. "This was only the beginning. If you behave well, I'm certain I will find some gentleman for you."

Julian's brow puckered at that, and he tossed his gloves aside.

I pretended to take Frances's words with confidence and return to my room, but instead I lingered on the stairs and listened for Julian and Frances to retreat to the drawing room. It was very wicked of me, but I was curious, so I snuck back down the carpeted stairs to hear what Julian said.

"Someone expressed interest in Athena?" Frances asked, her voice muffled by the closed door.

She needn't have sounded quite so surprised. But I was curious, too. I leaned closer.

"Lord Neale," my brother said, his voice weary.

A thrill of surprise and fear shot through me.

"Why is that name familiar?" Frances asked. "I can't place it."

"He is the one who some say murdered his sister last year."

There was a long pause, and my pulse quickened.

"That's excellent news!" Frances said.

I gawked at the closed door.

"Excellent news that a suspected killer wants to be acquainted with my sister?"

"Yes. Oh, don't worry. He's a lord. I'm sure he didn't actually kill her. But he is touched by scandal, too. It will be difficult for him to find a wife. Even if he did kill his sister, it would be far too suspicious for his wife to die mysteriously as well."

I rolled my eyes. Thank you, Frances, dear.

Another long, long pause. "That is…some comfort, I suppose."

"Certainly, you didn't turn him down."

Julian sighed. "I did not. Athena has always been competent. I was going to let her make the decision."

"Don't give her too much rein. We must arrange a meeting between them. Encourage her to accept him."

"There is a party in a few days. If we attend, he will be there to…look her over."

Oh, charming. Looked over like a horse at a racetrack. And by a potential murderer? I turned Mother's ring on my little finger. If only I took after her. I had admired her from afar as I dwelt in the nursery and she in her world of parties and balls. She was like a lovely doll on a shelf that I was not allowed to touch. If I had been her, men would have loved me despite the scandal. I would not be reduced to potential murderers as suitors.

I took a deep breath. That was unfair. If this Lord Neale was not judging me based on the rumors about my father, I should not judge him based on gossip either.

Of course, the rumors about my father were true. What if the same could be said of Lord Neale?

CHAPTER 3

The day of the party arrived, and Julian and Frances still hadn't admitted their scheme.

"I'll send my lady's maid to arrange your hair," Frances said. "Not that your maid isn't...competent, but there might be interesting gentlemen at this gathering, and we want you looking your most acceptable."

I kept my eyes down and murmured my thanks. When I shot my maid Jane an apologetic look, she had her gaze fixed on the carpet as well, her expression blank. After all, we were all dependent on Frances's fortune—and therefore her whims.

Jane silently helped me into my gown, a soft rose pink instead of the usual stark white. I studied myself in the mirror. My governess's mocking words still trampled through my mind as sharp as the first time I heard them. *You want your mother? Well, she has no time for you. Can't you see she only loves beautiful things? That is what vanity does to a woman. You must focus instead on being practical and respectable.*

Thanks to Father, I had failed at being respectable, leaving me only with practical.

Yet I harbored a secret guilty happiness that the soft pink of the gown brought some color to my face, and I did indeed look acceptable. I intended to give Lord Neale a chance. Frances did not want me. Society did not want me. Maybe someone who understood the weight of gossip would be able to look past it. Love was a glittering star I could not touch, but I might still find respect. I was, after all, named after the goddess who was wise and not at all romantic.

Frances hovered while her maid did her best to coax my hair into tight curls. The scent of the thick pomade and fire-heated papillote iron filled the room as the maid deftly fashioned the curls, wrapped them in curling papers, and baked them into submission.

The maid pulled the papers away, revealing tight spirals of brown hair.

Frances nodded her approval. "Now for some feathers."

"Must I?" I asked, trying not to sound petulant.

"You need every advantage you can get," Frances said, arranging several plumes in my hair. "But never fear—I will take care of all."

I winced as she added another feather. I would barely be able to move my head for fear of dislodging one or tickling the noses of anyone taller than me.

My brother gave me a sympathetic look when I came down the stairs, but we both knew there was nothing for it.

The house party was on the Circus, near the Upper

Assembly Rooms, so we once again took sedan chairs through town. We passed an elderly night watchman hobbling along with his lantern. No wonder highwaymen felt free to stalk the roadways.

The swaying back and forth of the sedan chair made me a little queasy, which I hoped would not ruin my fine color. If it did, I reminded myself, at least I still had a small dowry and a willingness to overlook rumors of murdered sisters.

The fine houses on the Circus ringed an open park and each had respectable gardens behind as well. Once, this level of luxury had been common for us. How I missed Mother's rose gardens.

Julian escorted us up the stairs to the front door, and from there a manservant showed us to the salon. I scanned the room, my heart beating faster than it ought to. Yet I did not see that dark-haired gentleman who had watched me at the Assembly Ball.

There was a great deal of card playing, which was not unusual, but the drinking and shouting and laughing were more than I thought decorous. We were a world away from the hallowed halls of Almack's, where once my mother had been hailed as diamond of the first water. The noise pounded against my skull.

"It's a little unruly," I whispered to Frances.

She wrinkled her nose. "Not every door in Bath is open to us, I'm afraid. You must not be fastidious. Don't let it bother you."

Not bother me? That we could only have admittance to less respectable parties? And that this was the type of place I was to find a husband. Perhaps it was the only party where

Lord Neale was admitted as well. Would that bother me? If I married someone shrouded in gossip, I would never escape it except by avoiding polite company. Of course, polite company hadn't done much for me thus far. Perhaps I was just as well without it.

Frances scanned the room, tapping her fan against her palm.

"Are you looking for someone?" I asked with feigned innocence.

Frances gave a guilty start. "What? No. I am only evaluating the company."

I did my best not to smile. Look what awkwardness your secret scheming causes, Frances, dear.

But my smile faded as the minutes ticked by and it became clear Lord Neale had not come. He must have learned more about Father. Obsessive gambling. Unpaid debts. Stealing from friends, from hosts, from other members of Society to try to wriggle free from the burden. Drinking himself to death before he could make amends or face justice. His children left to face the debts and the shame.

Thank goodness Frances had honored her engagement to Julian and brought her own fortune with her. We would owe her for the rest of our lives.

I waved my fan, trying to cool my burning cheeks. What did I care if Lord Neale spurned me? It was just as well since he might be a killer. What did I care if every man spurned me? I would become a lady's companion and live a quiet, respectable, easily forgotten life. I fanned faster, drying any silly tears that dared sting my eyes.

Young men laughed too loudly over their card game. One slammed his hand on the table, and I jumped at the bang.

Many in the crowd cast narrowed, speculative eyes at Julian. Was he going to play cards? To drink? *It runs in families, haven't you heard, the addiction to gambling and excess, to vice and dishonesty, everyone says once the bad blood shows itself you'll never breed it out, and it's a shame about the children, especially when the poor mother was such a beauty, but they'll take after the father, and there's nothing to be done for them, they're tainted, everyone knows, everyone knows, everyone knows...*

"Athena, you look pale," Julian whispered to me.

I gasped. "I...I need a moment of air."

I hurried away from my brother and the over-loud party and the scene of my further rejection.

Outside on the back steps, the darkness wrapped around me, hiding me from curious eyes. The noise from the party spilled out after me, but I ignored it. I rubbed my arms and stared up at the stars twinkling across the blackness. Impulsively, ridiculously, I plucked off one glove and reached my bare fingers for the sky as if I could touch its velvet softness.

The white roses in the garden caught my eye, almost glowing in the faint light from the house. White roses had been Mother's favorite. Roses that bloomed again after the first flush of summer were a novelty, only for the wealthiest gardeners—most from botanists finding new roses in the East Indies. I had rarely seen any. I shouldn't wander the gardens alone at night, but the temptation was too much, and I crunched over the gravel path to inhale their rich musk scent. I caressed the petals, each as delicate as fine porcelain, but they fluttered to the ground at my touch.

I stepped back and winced at a sharp pain in my foot. A gravel pebble had worked its way into my slipper. I sat on a bench to shake it out and heard footsteps approaching. My heart gave a lurch. Best not to be noticed, especially not alone in such a vulnerable situation. Not with my family's reputation for scandal. I pulled my slipper back on and crept behind a bronze statue of Artemis standing guard over her wild domain.

The interloper sat on the bench, whistling to himself. Out of tune. I groaned inwardly and settled against the cold statue for an unknown length of discomfort.

The stranger bolted to his feet, and my chest tightened. Had I been discovered?

But the footsteps retreated down the path. I slowly blew out my breath. I would be alone again soon.

"Oh, good evening." The stranger's voice made me start, but he wasn't talking to me. "I didn't... Um, what brings you here?"

He sounded nervous. Guilty. Perhaps I wasn't the only one who shouldn't have been in the garden that night.

A low murmur replied. I could not identify the speaker. They exchanged whispered words. Secrets spoken under starlight.

"What?" The first stranger nearly shouted. "No! Why would you think— What are you doing? Help!"

A gunshot blasted through the night. Something large hit the ground. I gasped and covered my mouth.

A dangerous stillness fell over the garden. Had the shooter heard me?

Footsteps moved slowly in my direction, a whisper against the gravel.

I pressed against the unforgiving chill of the statue, my pulse thrumming in my ears.

The footsteps paused near my hiding place. I could almost feel the shooter's eyes scanning the dark, noting the statue. Another step in my direction, the crunch of gravel grating up my spine.

I held my breath.

The next step was quieter, the footfall of a cat ready to pounce on its mouse.

My fingers trembled. I could not die like this, shot in a garden. It would be the ultimate scandal. A victory for the gossipmongers. A lonely, forgotten grave. Never respected, never loved. No, I had to flee. Hedges lined the planting beds, tall enough to hide me. I gathered my skirts, wincing at the faint swoosh of muslin, and dashed for the nearest one.

A bang broke the silence. Something buzzed near my ear and exploded through the hedge. A broken feather flopped into my face. Frances's cursed plumes were giving me away.

I ducked behind the hedge, my throat too dry to swallow. I yanked some of the feathers free and risked a glance back at the figure. It stalked in my direction, a cloak billowing around it, the light from the house throwing long shadows to trail it.

Certainly, someone would have heard the gunshots. The sound still rang in my ears. But the party in the house was loud. And with only an elderly night watchman patrolling and calling the hour, anyone wise would stay inside and ignore any trouble in the streets.

Sweat broke out on my forehead despite the cool of the night. Energy surged through my limbs. I needed to make it inside. I ducked my head and raced behind the hedges toward the house.

"Halt there!" From the direction of the street came a new voice, one I vaguely recognized.

I continued my scurry for the house.

Another gunshot rang out, this one from the newcomer. I risked a peek over the hedge and saw the cloaked figure pause and glance my direction. I lowered my head and peered between flimsy branches. The cloaked figured looked once more at the newcomer, then fled into the night.

The newcomer walked into the light from the house. It was the highwayman in his familiar mask, his pistol raised. A nervous giggle rose in my throat, but I clamped my mouth shut. Of all the people to save me. I slowly stood so he could see me and—hopefully—not shoot.

He spotted me and lowered his gun. "You! What are you…"

His gaze moved to something on the ground.

"No!" He sprinted in the direction of the body.

I looked about to confirm no one from the house had come out. We were still alone. I walked up around the hedge and came out a safe distance behind the highwayman, the refuge of the house within sprinting distance.

The highwayman crouched over the body on the gravel walk. The murdered man. My legs trembled. I forced myself to walk closer, to see the results of the encounter I'd over-heard. It seemed a form of justice to provide a witness. The dead man's face still wore a look of surprise. Blood darkened the path. I swallowed the taste of bile.

The highwayman studied the body intently.

"Did you know him?" I asked softly.

The highwayman swore under his breath. "Tell me what happened."

I refused to be shocked by his swearing or his abruptness and told him what I had heard.

"Did the dead man speak a name?" he asked.

"No."

More grumbled curses. "Did you see the shooter?"

"Only in outline. I could not identify him."

"You're certain it was a man?"

The question surprised me, but I considered it. "I believe so. He did not have the form or movements of a woman."

"That's something, at least." He groaned and rubbed his forehead above his mask. "And he saw you."

The statement sent a rush of cold over me. "Probably not clearly. I could not see him."

"Because of the cloak. You are very identifiable in the light from the house. Especially with those confounded feathers announcing your location."

"I should..." I swallowed. "I should go inside. Raise the hue and cry."

"Yes, and draw attention to yourself as the only witness."

"I can let it be known that I did not see the killer's face. I don't know anything. Then I will be safe."

He studied me for a moment, his eyes hard to read behind his mask. "Did you know the man who was killed? Were you in the garden for an assignation?"

I almost laughed at the absurdity. "Not at all. I'd never met him."

"He was here to give me information. A clue—only a hint—to help me answer a pressing question. The killer shot him for it. Do you think such a person will let you go? He will try to identify you, and when he does, he will silence you."

My bravado deflated. "Well, what do you expect me to do?"

The highwayman stood silently, studying me. Still, I could discern nothing of his expression, only see his keen eyes behind the mask. "Would you trust your brother to keep you safe? I certainly would not."

Julian had not been at his best when the highwayman robbed us. He had not been at his best since Father died. "I... Probably not."

"Is there someone else who can protect you? Perhaps someone who lives far from Bath and will offer you shelter?"

I lowered my head. "N-no." The word and the shame of it stuck in my throat. I had no one.

The highwayman paced and looked off into the distance. Then he chuckled softly and turned back to me. "What a situation, but I can't think of any other way..."

"What?" I asked, trying not to sound too despairing.

"I believe I am the only one who can protect you until we solve this dilemma."

"You will be my body-guard?" My spirits lifted for a moment, but then I shook my head. "That would look strange, to have an unrelated man always at my side." A highwayman at that. Especially since Frances wanted me to mingle and find a husband. And the highwayman could not follow me about at home. When I slept. My face warmed. "You must have better ways to spend your time, and I can't imagine my brother approving."

"We won't give him a choice. I will be your husband."

I stared at him for a moment, then laughed. "I don't even know who you are."

A smile flashed in his eyes. "If you marry me, I promise to tell you."

"I would certainly hope so! You truly expect me to agree to such a scheme?"

"It would keep you safe and protect your reputation. It might even draw the killer to you—and therefore to me. I'm not proposing a, um, full marriage. You could have it annulled later and still be accepted in Society."

I wasn't accepted in Society now. "Why would you go so far to protect me?" Then I remembered what he had said about searching for answers, drawing the killer out. "Oh. You want me to help you bait a trap."

"Perhaps, though I don't want anyone hurt because they stumbled into my affairs." He stepped closer and reached out as though he would hold onto me. "At the moment, you are the closest link I have to this killer."

"I didn't see his face."

"But you saw his form. You might recognize him if you encountered him again. It is a matter of life and death—of honor—that I find him, and you are now my best hope. I can't risk losing that. Losing you."

The words struck me in the chest. But it wasn't *me* he wanted, it was the vague images in my mind of a murderer. "Are you certain you can keep me safe?"

His jaw tightened, and he was silent for a long moment. "I will die before I let harm come to you. I give you my word."

His serious tone sent a thrill through me. Then the full danger of my situation settled in, and gooseflesh prickled up my arms. Someone wanted to kill me. Could I really consider marrying this stranger?

"You're not a mere highwayman, are you? You weren't born to the criminal life. You have the polish of a gentleman."

He gave a mock bow. "A gentleman by some definitions. I will keep my word like one—in fact, better than most. I assure you that marriage to me will not degrade your social standing."

A hot wave of self-consciousness washed over me, and I lowered my eyes. "You should know that the shadow of scandal hangs over my family. If you are respectable, their reputation might harm your name."

He laughed and gestured to his mask and garb. "Do I appear to care for reputations?"

I couldn't help chuckling. "I suppose not." I wet my lips. "If I agree to your scheme, what happens next?"

"Are you yet twenty-one?"

"Several years past," I admitted. On the shelf.

"Excellent. Then we can be married by license and avoid spreading your name abroad through banns. I hope you won't object if it's only a common license. I'm not inclined to ride to London for a special one."

He did have money and connections if he could obtain a special license. I nodded for him to go on.

"I will insist to your brother that you travel ahead to my

home—tomorrow—to prepare for the wedding. That will safely remove you from Bath while I stay behind to make preparations and hunt for the killer. I'll have my valet Walters keep a close eye on your home tonight."

"Your valet...who carries a blunderbuss?"

His eyes lit with a grin. "That's the man. He has many talents. You have a maid who can accompany you?"

"I believe I do." Jane would probably be glad to escape Frances, but I would not force her into a madcap plan.

I was considering it—this entire scheme. It was...practical? Was anything practical in such a situation?

As I stood in thought, the highwayman replaced his pistol in its holster and dragged the man's body out of sight. I shuddered and looked away.

The highwayman returned to me. "They'll discover him later, but this should make it less likely that anyone connects the death with either of us."

Us. We were bound together now by that terrible incident. I stared at the dark spot staining the pale gravel. I did not want to be the next victim of the cloaked killer.

"Why did you return my ring?" I asked.

He studied me, his gaze dark behind the mask. Then he shrugged one shoulder. "I could see its value to you was sentimental. It had no practical use for me."

"Why do you do it?"

A smile played in his eyes. "Perhaps one day I'll tell you."

I took a deep breath. "Very well. I agree to your plan. But you must show me your face."

"There's no turning back once you see me. My secret must remain safe."

"I understand."

He nodded and pulled off the mask, revealing himself as Lord Neale.

CHAPTER 4

"You!" I stepped back from Lord Neale, my pulse thundering in my ears.

He bowed with a flourish, and his lips twisted in a sardonic smile. "I warned you—it's too late to retreat. I'll sue you for breach of contract if you change your mind."

"Change *my* mind? I only attended this party because you told my brother you wanted to 'look me over.' And then you didn't even have the courtesy to appear."

He looked taken aback for a moment, then he stared down at the mask in his hand. "I'm certain I never suggested anything as crass as 'looking you over,'" he said quietly. He tucked the mask out of sight beneath his coat. In a more careless tone, he added, "I told your brother I would like to make your acquaintance. After our lively encounter on the road outside of Bath, I thought it would be amusing to converse again. I had no intention of burdening you with unwanted attentions. But I planned to join the party once my business here was done."

I closed my eyes. What had I done? Engaged myself to a man accused of murdering his sister—one who was also a highwayman. At least in my few interactions with him I didn't find him controlling or violent. Perhaps losing his sister and being accused of the crime had broken his mind. The information he had sought from the dead man might have been about her death. I could well imagine that. He might even fancy himself avenging her somehow, but I failed to see how highway robbery would clear his name or catch the real killer.

It wasn't to be a true marriage, at any rate. He hadn't wanted to "look me over" as a potential wife. He had only wanted amusing conversation. He would certainly get more than he bargained for, then. We both would.

I took a slow breath and opened my eyes to find Lord Neale watching me, his expression guarded.

"Very well," I said. "We should...break the news to Julian and Frances."

"Indeed."

Neale offered me his arm, and I took it gingerly. He set off for the house at a quick pace, and I had to tighten my grip or risk being left behind.

Inside, the house stank of sour wine and sweat, and the men and women were too engrossed in laughing, flirting, and cards to pay us much mind. Julian looked pained, and he glanced at times toward the front corridor. An ache rose in my throat. At least my brother wouldn't have to endure any more rude parties now.

Frances spotted our approach and gawked. A flicker of satisfaction glowed through the turmoil in my chest. Yes, Frances, dear, I wasn't as undesirable as you supposed. Even if my appeal was as bait in Lord Neale's trap.

She tugged on Julian's sleeve. His eyebrows rose, and then he narrowed his eyes at Lord Neale.

"Felicitate us," Neale said to them. "Your sister and I have had a delightful conversation, and she has agreed to become the next Lady Neale."

Frances's lips parted at the title, and she regarded me almost hungrily. "Who would have ever imagined our Athena as a baron's wife?"

"I would like a moment to speak to my sister," Julian said.

He pulled me aside, wincing at a loud outburst of laughter and swearing from a nearby card game. "You… you've agreed to marry Lord Neale? Despite the rumors about him?"

"The rumors about *us* don't leave me many options," I reminded him gently. "And after conversing with him, I don't think him guilty of the things people say."

Julian met my gaze. "That is good, but… You're not doing this for the title, are you? I know our situation is difficult, but I would not want you to have to make the kind of sacrifices…" He glanced toward Frances. "Well, I would like you to be happy."

Poor Julian. His concern warmed me, though it could do little else. I forced a smile. "I believe that on the most important points, Lord Neale and I are in harmony."

For instance, neither of us wanted me murdered, and, I

admitted to myself, I also would like to see the killer brought to justice.

Julian nodded, relief washing over his face. Yes, he no longer needed to concern himself about me. He would have enough of his own trials.

We returned to where Lord Neale and Frances stood, the former toying with a watch on a fob, the latter almost quivering with triumph. When we annulled the marriage and I became an anonymous lady's companion, Frances would not look so smug.

"I offer you congratulations for winning my sister over," Julian said, eyeing Lord Neale warily. "She is of an age to make her own choice, but you also have my blessing."

Lord Neale bowed his head and tucked the watch into his waistcoat pocket. "Excellent. I am not a patient lover, and I wish to act immediately. I intend to send your sister ahead of me to my estate at Briarwood. You and I can arrange the marriage settlement, then I will obtain a license and we will marry there quietly in a week's time."

Julian glanced at Frances. "We will see if we can make arrangements to travel—"

"There will be no need," Lord Neale said. "My servants will transport her belongings, and I intend the marriage to be a private affair. I am still in mourning, and I'm certain you understand the desire not to be gawked at. We will invite you to visit someday, of course, but it may be some time before you see your sister again."

A flash of alarm shivered through me at the finality of his decision, but if the killer was hunting me, we didn't want many people coming and going.

Julian opened his mouth, shut it again, and glanced at me.

"I will write," I assured him.

Frances nudged Julian. "We will send her with a maid, and Lord Neale is not staying at his estates with her. I'm certain all will be well."

Julian wrinkled his forehead, but after a reassuring smile from me, he nodded.

"To avoid painful rumors about your sister," Neale added, "I will request that you not spread word of our arrangement. After the marriage, you may publish all the announcements you wish."

Frances's eyes widened slightly. Ha, what a dilemma for her. A week without being able to brag or gossip! But it would be followed by a lifetime of dropping the name of her sister the baroness and finally being rid of her unwanted family member. She nodded, and Julian shrugged in defeat.

Lord Neale promised to see us first thing in the morning, and then we were free from that terrible party.

I hunkered down in the sedan chair's box for the trip home. A cloaked man waited out there in the night to silence me. To *kill* me. I jerked my head to see every movement on the edge of my vision. Was that a dark cloak? The flash of light off a gun barrel? No, only a cat darting from an alley. My pulse thrummed in my ears.

A shadow followed my sedan chair, stalked along beside it. It must be my imagination. No, there was a figure following. Cold rushed down my arms, freezing my fingers. I fumbled for the side of the chair, ready to scream. But the man glanced at me and nodded, lifting a blunderbuss so I could see it. The highwayman's henchman. Lord Neale's valet Walters. My fiancé worked quickly.

I leaned back against the chair, my hands shaking. I took slow breaths, allowing my shoulders to relax.

Once we were inside, Frances flung her mantle to a waiting maid and spun to face Julian.

"I knew I would triumph in Bath," she crowed. "The money, all the effort on Athena, and now we have a connection to a baron. Briarwood! It must be a grand estate. This will be a great thing for our family."

Julian tossed his gloves aside and gave me a worried look. "We will not see our new baroness or her estate for some time, I believe."

"Oh, don't be ridiculous. Lord Neale will tire of their honeymoon quickly enough, and then he will welcome company."

On that charming thought, I took myself off to my chamber. My chamber for one last night. Then, I was to face Briarwood. It would not be so terrible. Lord Neale did not love me, might not even care about me, but he would not be cruel. I would be locked away from the world, but that would keep me safe, and I did not care much for a world that didn't care for me.

Of course, I would be married to Lord Neale. I might have our marriage annulled someday and live in peaceful and semi-respectable retirement—I might still become a lady's companion—but I was unlikely to have another opportunity for marriage. And now, when every chance was gone, I had to admit that I had hoped. Something tore at my chest, like a jolt ripping open a scabbed-over wound. I sat heavily, not seeing, and the edge of the hard wooden chair bit into the back of my legs.

Which was worse: the uncertainty of dreaming of love that never came, or the certainty of a future that would never include love? Hot tears formed in my eyes.

Foolish Athena. I wiped my eyes dry. This was not practical. I pressed my hand against the ache in my chest and forced myself to be calm. This was my future, and I would make the most of it.

Jane half stumbled into my room, her eyes tired. She was not an energetic young girl anymore, being a few years older than myself. She'd been with our family as long as I could remember, always respectful and hard-working. She had enough intelligence and dignity that I selected her to serve as a lady's maid when I needed one and Father was too distracted to hire someone experienced. I couldn't imagine that Jane would enjoy being under Frances's charge once I was gone.

She glanced at my face with a worried pucker of her forehead, then went to work on my gown. She stifled a yawn as she worked the laces loose.

"Would you like to leave my brother's employ?" I asked her.

She straightened. "No, miss! I'm sorry for being inattentive."

I winced. "That's not what I meant. I'm getting married in a week. I'm leaving tomorrow. And I will take you with me if you like."

Her fingers paused over tugging at my laces. "Truly?"

"I'm marrying Lord Neale." I heard myself say the words,

but they sounded as though they had drifted in from some strange dream.

"Lord Neale!" Jane studied my face, looking for a jest. "But... Miss, I've heard other maids talk about him."

"Because of his sister? I don't believe the rumors."

"Not just that." Jane pressed her lips together, piquing my curiosity. Maids heard so much. She leaned closer. "They say his estate is cursed. Haunted, perhaps. Some of the maids who worked there have vanished."

That gave me pause. The woman at the ball had also mentioned a curse. "They vanished?"

"Run off, perhaps, driven mad, never to be heard from again. No one wants to work at that estate of his, Briarwood. Strange things happen there."

I squeezed my eyes shut. Rumors. Only rumors. Certainly, maids tended to exaggerate when they shared gossip.

"You do not have to come," I said wearily. "I will write you excellent references if you would rather not work for Frances."

Jane met my eyes in the mirror, watching me with a speculative frown. "No, miss. I think if you're determined to go, I'd better go with you. You've been good to me, and you shouldn't face the curse alone."

Not alone. Jane's words made me feel that perhaps I could face curses and Briarwood and even Lord Neale.

CHAPTER 5

I arose in the morning to find Jane all aflutter, folding the last of my gloves and shawls into my trunks. The sun coming through the window was still soft, half-asleep, and the early birdsong outside was not yet drown out by the grinding of a multitude of carriages on the street.

"I'm sorry to wake you, miss," she said. "But he's here."

"Lord Neale? Here already?" My sleepy pulse quickened, and I threw off my blankets.

He was not taking any chances that the killer might find me, then. Few people would even be awake this early in Bath —few of the upper class, at least. *Was* the murderer a so-called gentleman? The man he killed had sounded like one. I would have to ask my betrothed if he had any guesses. Working together, we would find the killer more quickly. I could be useful to him. He would not love me, but at least he would not despise me.

Jane's eyes sparkled. "Yes, miss. I saw him. I would say the devil's in that smile of his, except that he rescued you."

"Rescued me?" I paused from splashing warm water on my face at the dressing table. Had I given my garden adventure away in my half-awake state when we packed my trunks the previous night?

"From this place," Jane said, lowering her voice and glancing over her shoulder as if Frances might be lurking there. Then she bobbed a curtsey. "My lady."

Oh, dear. She didn't know this marriage was only for appearances. She thought she was going to be lady's maid to a baroness on a permanent basis. I would have to find a way to soothe her disappointment.

Jane helped me dress, fussing over my curls. I watched in the mirror as she made me presentable. Pretty, even? No, I couldn't count on that. My knee bounced as I tried to sit patiently. It didn't matter if I wasn't beautiful. Lord Neale only cared that I could help him find the killer. But Jane wouldn't understand that.

I was finally able to hurry downstairs, where I found Frances fawning over Lord Neale in the drawing room. My stomach turned like a rag being wrung dry at the sight. She looked so pleased with herself, a strutting, preening peahen. I couldn't imagine he was entertained by her, but he bore her prattling with a distracted air, glancing occasionally at his watch on its fob. At least it wasn't the fob he'd stolen from Julian. If only Frances knew he was the highwayman who had stolen her jewels... But of course, she never could know. She would not keep that secret.

While I watched him, I saw what Jane meant: there was something keen and sharp behind his bored smile. My betrothed wore more masks than just the highwayman's.

He glanced up as if he sensed my gaze. Our eyes met, and a shock of connection raced through me. For a moment, his eyes brightened, and the corner of his mouth lifted. Then, his politely disinterested expression fell back into place. My chest tightened, but I forced a smile.

Frances pouted when she noticed me. Lord Neale rose quickly and came to my side, taking my hand. It was only a performance for Frances, but it did reassure me. This was not a strange dream, and Lord Neale would protect me from the killer.

"Did you make certain the footman brought all your trunks down?" Frances asked me. "Oh, never mind. I will see to it as always."

My skin flushed at her tone, but I held my peace until she left the room.

"I am more competent than Frances would have you believe," I whispered to Lord Neale.

"I know it. I saw you on the road to Bath, if you recall." He flashed a smile—a real smile.

"Oh, of course," I said. He hadn't dropped my hand, and it gave me confidence to go on. "I wondered... do you think the man you're seeking is a gentleman?"

He looked surprised for a moment, then he released my hand. "Do not trouble yourself about it."

"But—"

"It's dangerous," he said. His ferocity startled me, but

then his expression softened again. "Don't fear—it's a short journey to Briarwood from Bath, and I will accompany you there and then return to arrange our marriage. You'll be safe from highwaymen on *this* journey."

I tried to smile at the joke, but my jaw was tense. How was I supposed to be of use if he wouldn't tell me anything?

As soon as the footmen appeared with my trunks, Lord Neale neatly took control of the situation from Frances. I barely had time to say goodbye to Julian before Jane and I were loaded in the carriage and rumbling away from Bath. No one could criticize Lord Neale on the condition of his equipage: the ride was much smoother leaving Bath than it had been coming. Jane looked as pleased as a chicken brooding on a clutch of eggs as she settled across from me and watched out the window. I curled my fingers into the buttery-soft leather of the cushioned seat as if I could stop this sudden tumble into an unknown future.

"I suppose we won't see any highwaymen with the baron riding alongside us," Jane said wistfully. "He is an excellent rider, is he not?"

I leaned so I could see, and I had to agree with Jane. Lord Neale carried himself well in the saddle. But then, a highwayman would have to, wouldn't he? It was his own coachman driving us, and I wondered how many of his servants knew of Lord Neale's clandestine activities. Probably only his valet. Such a secret would not stay concealed long if too many knew.

We traveled long enough for Jane and I to both doze off, and I awoke only when the pace of the carriage slowed. I peered out the window and found Lord Neale riding beside us.

He gestured for me to pull back the window coverings, and I did so.

"You'll catch a glimpse of Briarwood just ahead," he said.

I looked where he pointed, and in a moment, a break in the trees allowed me a look of my new home—however temporary it might be.

I had imagined Briarwood as an ancient castle crumbling down a cliffside. In fact, it was a solid, classical-styled building with columns and symmetrical rows of windows, probably no more than 200 years old, in good repair and surrounded by a pretty park.

"You're frowning," Neale said. "You're not pleased with Briarwood?"

His tone was light, but I sensed an undercurrent of concern.

"It looks very respectable."

He smirked. "Unlike its owner?"

I flushed. "I did not mean that! Only, I'd heard it was… haunted." That was more delicate than saying it was cursed.

He shrugged. "Every respectable old house has its specters, do they not?"

"Are you laughing at me?"

"I am laughing at the servants and the stories they tell. It's all stories—only stories. How can they hurt you?"

I scowled and settled back in my seat. Even Jane looked a bit put out by Lord Neale's comments.

Yet as we rode up the long drive to the house, the trees leaned close to the carriage, and branches not yet clothed in leaves reached out like supplicating fingers. The shadows hung deep and dark beneath the trees. The moss wrapping the trunks spoke of places where sunlight never touched.

I shivered and turned my gaze back to the house. Those many windows stared back like watching eyes. Every moment we drew closer, the feeling grew that the house—or something in it—was waiting for me. A cold lump settled in my stomach.

We reached the entrance, and Lord Neale helped me from the carriage. I stumbled a little—my legs stiff after sitting for so long—and grasped his hand for balance. He squeezed back, and I looked into his face, his eyes catching mine for a moment. Before I could make sense of what I saw there, he dropped my hand and turned to help Jane.

Only a handful of servants came forward to greet us. This was the staff, then. Not a large one—the only people willing to stay in a place rumored to be cursed?

Jane oversaw the unloading of my trunks, while Lord Neale guided me inside.

I halted in the entrance hall. Swirls of color and movement kept my eyes roaming around the high-ceiling room until I felt dizzy. The outside of the building was cool and classical, but the inside was a wild blend of baroque and rococo, alive with blues and golds. Richly painted figures paraded around the ceiling in a dance of the four seasons. Gilded vines climbed the columns lining the walls and coiled along the crown of the room. A staircase rose before me, pausing at a landing before splitting and curving into two separate wings of the house.

As I stared, I realized carved faces peeked out from

among the vines—devilish-looking cherubs with round cheeks and menacing smiles. They also glared at me from the posts of the staircase. Even the eyes of the figures painted on the ceiling were turned toward me, glaring, menacing. I curled my shoulders in and pulled my shawl tighter.

"I know," Lord Neale said, guiding me to the staircase. "It's terribly outdated and overdone, but my sister adored it. I haven't touched it."

I noticed that he did not expect me to make any changes. I supposed he hoped to find the killer before I had much time to settle in here. The marriage would be annulled, and this would all be a strange dream.

We walked up the stairs and paused on the landing where the staircase split.

"What's down that way?" I asked, pointing to the right.

"That's the family wing. You won't go there." He gestured left. "You have all of the guest wing to yourself. Plenty of space. We need not disturb one another."

He turned to leave.

A thrill of fear shot through me. I didn't want to be *too* close to this near-stranger, but I also didn't want to be alone in a house that spied on me through hundreds of carved and painted eyes. And at least when Lord Neale acted as the highwayman, I felt surprisingly safe with him.

"My maid will find it strange when I stay in the guest wing after the wedding," I blurted.

Lord Neale turned back to me, his gaze curious as it took in my face. I flushed under his scrutiny, and my pulse picked up. He stepped closer and lifted his hand as if he would grasp mine.

Then he sighed, and his mask of indifference fell back into place. "Tell her whatever you like. Tell her that my wing is haunted, and you don't wish to stay in it."

"My lord..." I said, wishing I could convince him to speak to me—to speak to me as the highwayman. Not to shut me out as everyone else did.

He looked back, his thoughts locked behind a neutral expression.

"Be careful," I said. "We know that man is dangerous."

"No harm will come to you," Lord Neale said. "Any servants who are left at Briarwood are very loyal."

"I would hate to see harm come to *you*."

He pressed his lips together, then gave me a bow. "You are too kind. The reputation of Lord Neale is in tatters, but no one shall doubt the goodness of Lady Neale. They will say you did your best to save me, but I was past all hope."

I gawked at him. Did he believe that? Before I could ask, he strode off to his wing of the house—where I was forbidden.

My governess's specter rose in my memory. I had been perhaps twelve and tried to make one of my brother's friends smile by flirting with my fan as my mother did. Miss Davidson snatched the fan from my grasp and hissed, "You will not charm anyone with your looks. They will only be impressed if you show them you are good and useful."

But Lord Neale would not let me be useful to him.

Jane hurried from the other corridor—the guest corridor —to find me.

"My lady! Your trunks are in your rooms, but I wasn't certain how much to unpack."

I strode up the remaining stairs to meet Jane and put on a smile. "I just spoke with my betrothed. He has gifted me this entire wing of Briarwood."

Jane looked confused by that.

I leaned closer. "He says any strange occurrences take place in the other end of the house, and he wants nothing to disturb me or make me dislike Briarwood."

Jane's eyes widened. "That is thoughtful! And it means the house really is haunted."

"Well, we shall be safe, at least. Will you show me which chambers are mine?"

"Of course, my lady!"

It would take some getting used to—hearing the title that would not really be my own. Just a borrowed gown for a pantomime show.

Jane led me down the corridor. Eyes watched us from the paintings and the carved columns and crown moldings.

"This one is yours," Jane announced. "The housekeeper gave me a room down the corridor, and we'll arrange a bell, so I won't be too far if you need me."

"Excellent." At least I was not entirely alone.

My antechamber and bed chamber were spacious and well-appointed, freshly aired and with a fire burning, though its warmth did not stretch far beyond the hearth. The room was still offensively Baroque, though it did not have as many watching faces as the entrance hall. One painting in particular sent another shiver through me: a swirling image of Hades carrying Persephone off to the underworld while satyrs laughed and danced. I would have to do something about that. The house might not be mine, but this room was for the moment.

We unpacked my trunks and aired and arranged my dresses until Jane decided it was time for supper.

When she left, I stepped back to study the distasteful painting, trying to decide how best to move or cover it.

Someone tapped on the door.

"Enter," I said.

A thin, almost bony lady with gray hair and an upright bearing stepped into the room.

"I'm Mrs. Harris, the housekeeper. My lord instructed me to introduce myself and await your instructions." She studied me like a ribbon in a shop window. It was very rude of a servant, but I could already see that this would not be a typical household.

I hesitated, gathering my words. This was an awkward situation, arriving as the soon-to-be lady of the house when I wasn't staying, and when the house had been running well without me interfering. Yet it would be odd if I did not try to take some charge over the household.

"I would like to see next week's menus as soon as it's convenient," I said. "Especially your plans for the wedding supper."

She nodded stiffly. "It would be bad luck not to have a bridal cake, and we don't want to bring any more bad luck to Briarwood."

"You've certainly had sorrow here in the last year."

"We're cursed," she said matter-of-factly.

My eyebrows rose. "You believe in the curse then?"

"Of course I do! I'm not a fool." She lowered her voice. "If you're wise, you'll believe and go before it's too late."

A shiver ran through me. "What will the curse do to me, then?"

"Who's to say? Sorrow follows those who come to Briarwood."

"Why don't you leave?" I asked.

"Who would take me? No one wants the castoffs of Briarwood."

I winced at that. "Then I suppose I have nowhere to go, either."

Harris's face softened a little. "At least you're not easily frightened."

"I suppose I should expect ghosts here as well?"

"Perhaps just the one."

I studied her expression—her face as stiff as the carved ones in the corridors, but her eyes sad.

Jane returned then with our supper tray. Harris said nothing else except to promise to bring me the week's menus to approve, then she exited.

When it was time for sleep, Jane helped me undress and left for her own room.

The emptiness of the house pressed around me. A clock ticked on the mantle, each loud click echoing in the enormous stillness of Briarwood. I thought of Lord Neale off in Bath or elsewhere and a killer somewhere hunting for me. I took two steps to rush after Jane and beg her to stay, but I stopped myself. Harris would no doubt discover it and think me a child or a coward. Maybe she would tell Lord Neale, and he would never allow me to be of any use. And all those watching eyes would see.

I bolted myself in, then glared at the painting of Hades. A lacquered dressing screen stood near the fireplace. It was heavy, and the polished smoothness made it difficult to grip. Nevertheless, I took hold and inched it over, my fingertips pressing into the unforgiving wood. I finally wrestled the screen into place in front of the offending painting. There! I shook out my sore fingers and smiled.

The near-silence greeted me again. As if the house was not just watching but listening. Waiting. Lord Neale kept no dogs that I had seen, and the few servants were either asleep or avoiding my wing. In the quiet, though, I thought I heard a faint whisper. Probably just the wind picking its way through loose windows and down corridors.

The wood of the door creaked.

I held my breath, watching to see if anyone disturbed the handle.

A light shone for a moment along the crack at the bottom of my door. Then it vanished, and all was quiet again except the ceaseless ticking of the clock.

I went cold and still as I stared at my door. Then a hot flood of anger poured through me. Was Harris or some other person trying to frighten me away? Even if it were some restless spirit, where else did it expect me to go? I had chosen this path, and I would see it through. It was only practical, after all.

I reached for the handle, ready with a tongue-lashing, but then I saw again the body of that poor man on the gravel path. The bang of the pistol echoed in my ears, and the scent of hot gunpowder filled my nose and throat.

No. I would not open that door. Not tonight. I might not be the true Lady Neale, mistress of Briarwood, but I would be mistress of my own destiny. After all, I had survived my father's scandal and even Frances. I checked the bolt again, put out the candles, and crawled through the bed curtains into the chilly blankets. Sometime in the deep stillness of the night, sleep finally claimed me.

CHAPTER 6

Morning light poked through the heavy damask bed curtains like prying fingers. I groaned and rubbed my eyes. Any moment, Frances would berate me for oversleeping.

I sat up. No. I never had to listen to Frances again. This was Briarwood. It was too much to hope that Lord Neale would want me to stay permanently, but if I proved myself useful and worthy of his aid, maybe he would help me find a suitable retirement.

To help Lord Neale, I needed to understand him—and Briarwood. I rose and pulled on my dressing gown, the thick wool rug cushioning my steps as I walked the spacious room. I needed to explore Briarwood, maybe poke into places I wasn't strictly invited. That meant going without Jane. She would be blameless if I incurred Lord Neale's wrath.

Her soft tap sounded on the door. The door I had bolted

in the night. By daylight, it was clearly a foolish thing to do. I hurried to let her in.

She carried in the breakfast tray, concern wrinkling her forehead. "This was outside the door. Did you lock it last night?"

A sign that I did not trust Lord Neale or his people to keep me safe. But Jane did not know about the killer in the garden.

"Oh, yes." I laughed lightly. "I was a little nervous in a new place."

Jane's eyes brightened. "So was I! Even if it is the other wing of the house that is haunted."

I lifted the breakfast cover and wrinkled my nose at the cold pigeon and lukewarm tea that awaited me. In fairness, it was probably warm when the cook sent it up. I picked at it while Jane sorted through my gowns, remembering the light I had seen outside my door.

As she helped me dress and arrange my hair, I asked. "Did anything disturb your sleep last night?"

"Not at all. I slept like the dead." Jane sighed wistfully. "I suppose hearing the weeping of some tragic spirit would not be as romantic if it interfered with our sleep."

"Not at all," I said with a shudder. "Let's think instead of the wedding."

"Yes?" Jane's face brightened.

"You know it will be a quiet affair. I think I would like to wear the pale pink dress." The one I'd been wearing when all this trouble started. The one that made me look passable.

"Oh, excellent choice. But it could use some new ribbons."

I nodded. "Just so. Can you see to it?"

"Of course, my lady! I understand there's a village only a couple of miles from here. It will have a shop and a selection of ribbons, I'm sure."

Jane gathered the gown and hurried from the room.

Now was my chance. I smiled and took the key to my room, the brass heavy in my hand, shutting the door quietly behind me.

Harris waited for me in the corridor, her long face as wooden as any carved into the banisters. I gave a start like a naughty child discovered stealing lumps of sugar in the kitchen. Blast the woman!

"I've brought you the menus," Harris said, extending several papers to me.

"Ah, yes." Perhaps I could be rid of her quickly.

I scanned the pages covered in prim handwriting. The menu wasn't elaborate, but Lord Neale didn't skimp, either. No cheap cuts of meat or dull gruels. This must mostly be for my benefit since he was not to be at the house for the next week.

"Very good," I said, handing the papers back to her. "Your cook enjoys using trout? I noticed a great deal of it."

Harris stared at me for a long moment, then she folded up the paper. "We have a well-stocked pond. It was *her* favorite."

No question who *she* was. And I doubted much chance of changing it, from Harris's stony expression. My shoulder blades itched as though someone were watching us, though I knew if I looked over my shoulder, the corridor would be empty. Trout wasn't my favorite, but I could stomach it. I sighed. Now I had a taste of what Frances had felt, moving into a house where another woman had already set the tone and the pace. And in this case, I was competing with a dead girl.

"You have other questions for me?" Harris watched me closely. "My lord wanted me to attend closely to you as you settle in."

I surrendered. "I had hoped to become better acquainted with the house today. Would you provide me a tour?"

This would be a start, and I would decide what to explore later on my own.

Housekeepers usually enjoyed showing off the estate, but Harris sniffed and studied me with suspicion. She reminded me of my despised governess in that moment, and I resisted the impulse to make certain my nails were clean.

"Very well," she finally said.

She turned on her heel and marched away, and I scrambled to follow. She rambled off facts about the house as she guided me through chambers and corridors: which ancestor was which in the portraits and which rooms had hosted notable visitors in past generations. We finished the guest wing and then visited the drawing rooms and dining rooms, all elegant in their swirling baroque grandness. All with carved and painted eyes that watched, questioning by what right a disgraced and castoff woman walked beneath their venerable gazes.

I struggled to focus, but when Harris seemed to expect it, I nodded and offered appreciative "ohs" and "hmms."

Finally, we ended in the ballroom. I needed no false

interest here. Gilded mirrors lined the walls, reflecting the light from the windows in a glittering display. Golden chandeliers held snuffed candles at the ready. The shepherds and nymphs that swirled around the ceiling stood frozen in their dance, just waiting for music to bring them to life.

My mother would have loved this room. She would have been perfectly at home in it. Dancing with admiring gentlemen, her gown swirling about her slippers, her eyes sparkling in the candlelight as she greeted guests. Her merriment only fading when her gaze found me hiding behind the curtains, watching like a besotted mortal who had stumbled into fairyland. And then Miss Davidson would whisk me away and scold me for being such a wicked, burdensome child.

You will only upset your mother by going where you're not wanted. You must be very good and maybe she will come see you in the nursery.

But the nursery was not a lovely place. My mother rarely came and never stayed long when she did, always seeming ill at ease.

I took a step back from the ballroom, clutching my hands to my squirming stomach.

Harris gave a little grunt, watching me with a furrowed brow.

I caught her eye and remembered myself. "It's beautiful."

Her face softened a little. "Yes. It's one of the finest rooms in the house. It was her favorite."

"I see." I studied the bright room again. "The neighborhood must look forward to balls hosted at Briarwood."

Harris's expression turned cold again. "There will be no more balls at Briarwood."

She turned her back on the ballroom and swished away. I scurried after.

She stopped in the entrance hall and glared at me, as though annoyed I had troubled her for this tour. Well, with a small household staff, I probably had interrupted her work, but I wasn't finished yet.

"And the other wing?" I asked, pretending innocence.

She narrowed her eyes. "Only the family goes in that wing."

I winced inwardly at that reminder that I did not belong—would never belong. She gave me a perfunctory curtsey and headed herself up the stairs and into the corridor that I was forbidden from entering. Perhaps to guard it from me.

I gritted my teeth, but what was I to do? I could not make myself too obnoxious to Lord Neale's servants or he might decide I was too much trouble and send me away into the clutches of the killer. I should not go where I was not wanted.

My gaze wandered to the entrance hall with its many watching faces. My chest felt tight, my hands cold. But sunlight poured in through the windows, warming my dress. The garden. No one had said I could not explore the garden. No eyes would judge me there. It likely wrapped around both wings of the house, giving me an opportunity to glimpse the mysterious rooms no one wanted me to see.

The corridor by the ballroom led to the back of the house. I snuck past the grand room and down the steps that took me outside.

I stopped on a stone terrace looking out over the landscape. A smile spread over my face. My father couldn't afford to follow the latest garden designs—nor did he care to after Mother died—but at Briarwood, the landscape had been lovingly tended.

The scene before me had been transformed into a series of terraces, starting with the stone one I stood on, descending to a level area of flower gardens with fountains and benches, then moving downward to a slow river and long, serpentine lake that was no doubt the source of the endless trout we would be consuming. A crumbling faux Roman temple stood on the shores of the lake, inviting me to look further to the wooded hills in the distance.

I picked my way down the stone steps to the flower gardens. A familiar scent caught my nose: Roses. In autumn! I thought again of Mother. The garden was not like the ballroom. She wore simple gowns and an easy smile in the garden and invited me to know the flowers and see to their needs.

Roses are the most beautiful flower—a symbol of love—but they do not do well with weeds growing at their feet. You must be careful though, because they'll grab you with their thorns.

My heart lifted as I wandered the paths between benches and flowers. This garden was carefully laid out but recently neglected. Gardens always needed extra work. They were constantly growing, changing, whether anyone paid attention or not.

I reached the rose garden and stifled a gasp. The Neales were collectors. They had not only the white autumn-blooming musk rose, but also several pink ones and a bright crimson I had never seen before. I tip-toed forward to sniff the delicate petals, their fragrance sweet and very different from the musks and damasks I knew. I cradled their velvety softness with my fingers, marveling especially at the bright crimson rose. How had the Neales acquired such a treasure? And why had such a rare thing become so neglected?

Oh, yes, this place needed me. The roses hadn't been trimmed back, and wilted petals clung to the bushes. Weeds sprung up among the flowers. I removed my delicate gloves and knelt to clear the weeds, moving carefully among the thorny branches. The roses breathed the sweet scent of their approval over me as I bent to work at their feet.

I could spend many happy hours in this garden, weeding, trimming, even working on my embroidery. There was a bench perfectly situated to catch the warm afternoon sun.

Among the prickly fallen leaves, a single pearl caught my eye. It must have come from some lady's ring or gown. I picked it up, not certain what to do with it, and finally dropped it into the finger of one of my neglected gloves.

I brushed off my hands and sat on the bench to let the sun wash over me. I closed my eyes and turned to face the sun. What did I care if I grew freckled? If there was dirt under my nails? No one here cared what I looked like.

With my eyes closed, I could imagine someone sitting next to me. A warm, friendly presence, as if the garden itself had a spirit that had grown lonely and was glad to have a visitor.

"What are you doing there?" Lord Neale's voice boomed.

I jumped to my feet, all sense of welcome evaporated, and turned to find him glaring down at me. My throat tightened. His dark hair was somewhat disheveled—probably from riding—and emotions flared in his deep brown eyes: anger and perhaps...fear?

"What are you doing back?" I asked, trying to keep my voice steady.

"I needed some documents for the marriage settlement," he snapped. "But what are *you* doing out here?"

"I wanted some fresh air. Must I always stay in the house?"

He looked away, his jaw tight. Slowly, he regained his mask of politeness. When he spoke again, the words were cool but level. "Of course not. You are free to wander down to the lake—but no farther or you will be out of sight of the house and...vulnerable."

Vulnerable to the killer should he discover my identity. "Would it not be safer to stay in these gardens, closer to the house, then? The flowers are overgrown. They need attention."

"No!" He stopped and squeezed his eyes shut, then spoke slowly. "It was my sister's, and no one else is to touch it. I cannot... I came up from the stables and saw..."

He rubbed his face and looked up to the house—to one of the windows in the family's wing. I realized what he had seen from the stables. A woman sitting in his sister's garden. Probably on her favorite bench. My heart swelled with sympathy.

"I apologize, my lord," I said. "I did not mean to alarm you. But would it not honor your sister if—"

"No. You may take the air on the lower terraces or down

by the lake, but you will stay away from this terrace—and especially the rose garden."

And with that, he turned and stormed back toward the house. I wanted to scream at him, but my chest was tight, almost too tight to breathe. One more area where I could not be helpful. One more bar in my cage. I should not go where I was not wanted—and I was not wanted anywhere.

CHAPTER 7

Afraid of offending my fiancé again, I resigned myself to spending the week with Jane preparing for the wedding—maintaining the facade. I put on a false smile and tried to act as happy as a real bride as we stitched my gown and planned the wedding feast. It needn't be a large feast. We didn't have a crowd of family or friends celebrating with us. The only thing to celebrate was that we had fooled the murderer so far.

But as I embroidered roses onto my white gloves, my mind drifted. What would it have been like to plan a wedding because someone wanted me? Someone who thought me so useful that he couldn't do without me. Maybe even a little pretty. Someone who looked at me with even a sliver of the adoration my father had shown my mother. Or even the way Julian looked at Frances before Father's scandal and death upended everything. To be wanted... to be cherished...

"You must be excited," Jane said. "You have a glow about you."

I gave a guilty start and dropped my stitch. What a foolish daydream! That sort of marriage was rare enough, and it was certainly not to be my fate. "Oh, well, of course I am. I don't know Lord Neale well, but…"

Jane nodded sagely. "But such arrangements are common, and you'll be settled comfortably for life."

Only if the murderer didn't find me. I had to stifle a laugh. Nothing about this was common.

"I'm sorry your mother won't see," Jane said softly.

That poured ice over my mirth, and I stared down at the gloves in my lap. "I'm sure she would have wanted something more…more fine than this quick marriage by license."

"Perhaps." Jane grinned. "If so, she would have charmed Lord Neale into whatever wedding she wished for you: A gown from London, a huge party for the wedding feast with an orchestra and dancing, and a bride cake with almond icing. She could charm a vicar out of his Bible if she wished."

I sighed. "That is no doubt true."

Though I suspected even my beautiful and clever mother would not have known how to manage the mercurial Lord Neale and his many masks.

"It's good luck to marry in September, though!" Jane went on. "'Marry in September's shrine, your living will be rich and fine.' Like being a baroness! It's a shame you can't be married on a Wednesday instead of a Thursday. 'Thursday brides will suffer losses.'" She frowned over that, then gave me a sly look. "Well, you're losing Frances. That's something to be grateful for."

I should have reprimanded her, but I couldn't help chuckling. Yes, I would make the most of this strange opportunity.

Thursday approached quickly, and before my new reality had become fully solid in my mind, Jane was helping me into my wedding gown.

I studied my reflection in the mirror and gave a nod of approval. Passable. The best I could hope for. My stomach fluttered. This was my wedding day, after all, and I was glad to look my best.

"You're beautiful!" Jane sighed. "Now, you must add your gloves to finish dressing and then not look in a mirror again or you'll have bad luck. Lord Neale has prepared his carriage to take us to the church."

I nodded. Lord Neale and I would not arrive together, as that would look very strange—respectable brides did not normally live in their husband's house before the wedding.

Jane handed me a bouquet. The sweet scent of roses filled my nose. They could only be from Lord Neale's forbidden gardens. I had not warned Jane to avoid them. I hesitated only a moment, then decided it would be silly to toss them away. And the white roses in particular reminded me of my mother, as if she were there with me. I clutched the bouquet. Hopefully, Lord Neale would not think anything amiss with flowers on a wedding day.

Jane led me downstairs, and we found the carriage awaiting us. The few male servants still in service at Briarwood stood in the entryway like guards at attention. The many carved and painted eyes of the house watched me pass. One of the manservants opened the door for me, and another handed me into the carriage, and then Jane after. I could not remember a time when so much attention had been focused solely on me, and it set my heart racing.

My pulse did not slow when we reached the church. I had no father to give me away, and I entered the church with only Jane as an escort. The church's interior was dark and cool compared to the bright autumn sun, and the stone faces of unknown saints and benefactors stared down impassively.

Lord Neale waited just inside the church doors. His suit was of fine black cloth and appeared new-made. Had he commissioned it for our wedding? As if he also wished to look his best. No doubt he only wanted to look respectable for the sake of appearances. He *was* sternly handsome, his clean-shaven jaw set stubbornly and his dark eyes guarded.

I smiled in relief at seeing a familiar face, and a grin briefly lit his expression, momentarily startled out of his mask of politeness. His face regained its neutrality, but he offered his arm and watched carefully as I took it. The solidness of his forearm beneath my fingers finally calmed my pulse. This day was real—and it would keep me safe.

He gave me a reassuring nod and guided me past the empty pews to the vicar waiting at the front, his wife serving as a witness. Jane quietly took a seat.

The vicar looked at me curiously, then cleared his throat and began. He read the ceremony with much feeling, extolling the virtues of marriage to the rafters, finally pausing at, "If any man can show just cause, why they should not be joined together, let him speak now or hereafter forever hold his peace."

I resisted the urge to look over my shoulder at Jane, because there was no one else in the church who could object. Maybe the vicar expected someone to burst in and protect me from the rumored beastliness of Lord Neale. He would be disappointed.

Lord Neale shifted in the silence.

The vicar cleared his throat and leveled at look at both of us, but especially at Lord Neale. "I require and charge both of you—as ye will answer at the dreadful day of judgement when the secrets of all hearts shall be disclosed—that if either of you know any impediment why ye may not be lawfully joined together in matrimony, ye do confess it now."

I couldn't help myself. I glanced up at Lord Neale. He met my eye, and I thought I caught a sparkle of humor there. After all, we had no prior marriages or close kinship to prevent us from engaging in a false marriage if we wished. The vicar didn't know the secret we shared, but I had to suppose that God did and would approve our reasons.

I thought I caught a little sigh from the vicar before he went on. I gave a start when he said, "Richard Neale, wilt thou have this woman to thy wedded wife?"

His name was Richard. I had only learned that at the altar. I bit my lip to prevent an inappropriate chuckle at the ridiculousness of the situation.

"I will," Richard said.

What had he just promised? To comfort and honor me? I didn't have time to try to remember, because now it was my turn.

"Wilt thou obey him, and serve him, love, honor, and

keep him in sickness and in health; and, forsaking all others, keep thee only unto him, so long as ye both shall live?"

I believed I could make that promise in good faith. Even if our marriage was annulled, I wasn't likely to marry another. And I wanted to serve and help him.

I felt Richard's eyes on me. I glanced up, caught his curious gaze, and my cheeks warmed.

"I will," I said.

I couldn't quite meet Richard's gaze as the vicar guided us through our vows to the blessing of the ring.

Richard placed the ring on my finger, his hand warm on mine. "With this ring I thee wed, with my body I thee worship, and with all my worldly goods I thee endow." His deep voice filled the church.

I met his dark eyes, trying to read what he was thinking. My heart wrenched, and I quickly looked down. They were lovely words, but they were not truly meant for me.

As the vicar prayed over our union, my eyes fastened on the gold ring on my finger. It was adorned with five little pearls around a garnet, forming a flower. I almost looked up to Richard again. Was he teasing me about the garden?

When the vicar finished the prayers, we signed the register, and in the eyes of the law, at least, Richard and I were husband and wife. I assumed God knew better.

Richard escorted me from the church. The bells rang out, and I startled at the sound.

"It's customary," Richard whispered—his first real words to me that day. "We would not want anything to seem unusual about the marriage. For that reason, a few neighbors will also be attending the wedding feast. They would be offended not to be the first to meet the new Lady Neale and would think something was amiss when word reached them I had married too secretly."

I nodded. His reasoning was sound. But the solemness of the ceremony and the duplicity of our arrangement weighed on me, and I found it hard to maintain my smile.

We returned together in the carriage, Jane suppressing a grin in the seat across from us.

Briarwood felt a little different as we stepped inside. A bit warmer, perhaps. A fiddler played in the dining hall—not Jane's imagined orchestra, but it was cheerful. The notes jarred against my feeling of uncertainty, reminding me I was an imposter. Likewise, the smiles on the first neighbors who arrived to greet me—a couple named Reeves—seemed too bright. Suspicious?

Mrs. Reeves was a handsome woman, the few lines beside her eyes adding a touch of dignity to a round, almost girlish face. Mr. Reeves was very round himself, and the too-familiar scent of gin on his breath turned my stomach.

"Our daughters will call on you soon, I have no doubt, Lady Neale," Mrs. Reeves assured me, patting my hand.

My smile twitched at the title.

She paid no heed. "They had already planned on being in Bath today for the ball. They do hate to miss a ball, and it was such short notice..." She raised an eyebrow and glanced at Richard. "But they regretted being absent for your celebration."

How strange that just over a week earlier, I had expected to be at that ball myself.

"Not much of a celebration for young people anyway," Mr. Reeves muttered.

He was correct. The fiddler was competent, but he did not play dancing tunes. The meal would include bread and roast beef and fruits from Briarwood's orchards but no exotic treats, and the bride cake had such a thick, cloying icing that the pieces sent home with guests would probably last for months.

The only guests to arrive besides the Reeves was a couple even older than them.

"Lady Neale," my husband said, holding my arm as if to fortify me in the face of his neighbors. "May I introduce Mr. and Mrs. Palmer."

I gave a start. I knew Mrs. Palmer. She was the one who had spoken to me at the Assembly Ball in Bath. She took my hand with a sly smile and greeted me as if we were strangers. There would be much travel between this neighborhood and Bath, with the distance being reasonable and little entertainment in the area. But a prickle of shock ran down my spine to see her again. Perhaps it was fate. She might hire me as a lady's companion after all when Lord Neale dissolved our marriage.

Mr. Palmer—a tall, gray-haired gentleman with an upright bearing at odds with his sagging wrinkles—greeted me with formal politeness. Then Richard led me past all of them to the head of the table.

Conversation over the meal was stilted. It was clear the guests were tiptoeing around any awkward questions. Some of those no doubt were about where Lord Neale had come across me so suddenly.

"Where is your family from, Lady Neale?" Mrs. Reeves asked. "I know so many families in Society, it's likely I've met them."

"They are from Bedfordshire," Richard answered. "They are not out in Society much."

He was careful not to mention Bath, but Mrs. Palmer gave me a conspiratorial smile. Once Frances was permitted to publish the wedding announcement, everyone would know the new Lady Neale was the disgraced Miss Ratliffe. At least I didn't have to face the shocked stares and awkward smiles today.

The conversation lumbered on. Not all of the stiffness could be attributed to my mysterious appearance at Briarwood or even Richard's reputation. Some of it must have come from *her*. One of the servants had set an extra place at the table—perhaps not an accident—and everyone's eyes darted to it from time to time. Richard's sister dominated every moment, every breath at Briarwood. I borrowed a trick from Richard and wore a polite mask through it all.

Finally, the guests left with their slices of bride cake, and Richard and I were alone.

CHAPTER 8

Richard was silent for a long moment after the last rumbles and jingles of our guests' carriages faded. My stomach fluttered as I waited for him to break the silence. He fidgeted with the cuff of his coat then finally met my gaze. He wore his polite mask again.

"I think that went well," he said. "The neighborhood will know we're married. If the murderer hears of it, he will not connect it to Bath immediately. It's unfortunate that the wedding announcement will give you away, but it can't be helped."

A shiver raced over my skin. "You think the murderer is watching you, then."

"I don't know," Richard said, "and so I'm cautious. You must be as well. Stay close to the house. Go no farther abroad than the pond. Receive guests when they come, but be wary of anyone who seeks out your acquaintance. Keep to yourself."

Like a prisoner. "I will have you to talk to at least. Won't I?"

I met his eyes, pleading.

His expression softened for a moment. "Perhaps, sometimes."

"I can help—"

He looked away. "I am poor company, as anyone will tell you. You have your maid Jane. You two may entertain each other. In the drawing-room, you will find cards, tables games, and a piano-forte."

"But—"

"Good night, Miss... Lady Neale."

He bowed and strode off, leaving me wanting to scream at him. Tables games! Cards! I would go mad with such useless pursuits.

Jane, who had been waiting respectfully out of earshot, appeared now, a huge grin on her face.

"Time to help you out of your gown and leave you to your wedding night," she said with a giggle.

Wedding night indeed! I felt like I might be sick, but I forced a smile, trying to play it off as nerves. "Yes, let's be away."

Jane smiled the whole time she helped me off with my gown, and then she slipped out, leaving me alone.

So very alone.

I pulled my dressing gown on and huddled on the sofa in my antechamber, trying to ward off the cold. My heart beat hard, each thump a painful blow in my chest, and my throat ached. I would always be alone. Useless. What good was I sitting in the drawing-room entertaining myself? I was never meant to be a decorative lady. Miss Davidson had made that clear. I was practical. Efficient. Nothing else. And if I was not those things, then I was nothing at all.

I buried my face in my hands. Could there be a worse torment than being cast off? I groaned, fighting the urge to scream or cry until oblivion swallowed me. I had to scratch, claw, fight my way to the surface like a drowning cat.

The only way out was to solve the mysteries of Briarwood and escape to some place where I could be useful. I had promised to obey Richard, but I had also promised to serve him. Despite Miss Davidson's best efforts, I had never been a *good* girl. Not truly obedient. My heart rebelled, some corner of it always wild. Certainly, service was more important than obedience anyway.

I raised my head, taking slow, deep breaths to push back against the weight in my chest.

When the corridors grew silent and still, I opened the door. Even Harris would avoid my chambers, expecting Richard to visit me. And Richard would no doubt stay far away. I couldn't explore his wing of the house, but I could see more of this wing without anyone hovering.

Portraits of Neale ancestors looked down on me as I walked the corridor, and I kept my gaze low until I came to the hall that joined the two wings of the house.

A faint glimmer of light down the stairs caught my attention. It seemed to come from one of the rooms—maybe the ballroom. Was someone there? Maybe a servant cleaning, though the house was deathly quiet.

What was I thinking? I was practical. Reliable. I stayed

out of the way. No one wanted me in the way—not at home, not here, never anywhere. I should only do what I had always done and behave myself and not cause trouble and dream that someday someone would think me worth looking on.

But if I was ever to go somewhere where I would be appreciated, I had to be free from Briarwood. So, I followed my curiosity and snuck down the stairs to investigate.

The lights indeed came from the ballroom, though no one was there and the candles were not lit. The glimmers hung in the air like stars captured and brought indoors. I could find no source for them. As I watched, they began to move. To sway. Almost as though they had been waiting for me.

My first instinct was to run, but I was frozen in place by the beauty of the lights. Was this part of the curse of Briarwood? Were the lights drawing me in only to snuff me out? For a moment, reveling in their beauty and wonder, I did not care.

The lights swirled into a pattern, like couples spinning around the room. There was no music that I could hear, but the lights pulsed to a distinctive beat, and I could almost tap my foot along with the joyous, soundless tune. It was...

It was a celebration as Jane had described. A wedding celebration. The lights swirled around me, too, inviting me to step inside. Like a person in a dream, I did. Stepped into the wonder of the lights twinkling around me, orbs of moonlight come to skim above the earth.

For a moment, I was a child again, watching my mother

dance. But this time, instead of a stern governess dragging me away, my mother beckoned me to dance with her.

I spun slowly, staring at the lights. Dancing with them. I spread my arms out, twirling, imagining I was not alone. Imagining someone—maybe someone with dark hair and dark eyes that were so difficult to read—dancing along with me. That I was loved and cherished. If I was dreaming, I could dream anything. I grew so warm and light, I could have flown around the room with the twinkling orbs.

The lights shone brighter as they shared my dance. Then they began to dim, the pulse of their music fading. They blinked out one by one until the ballroom was dark and still. I spun to a stop and let the blackness roll around and swallow me, reveling in the silent anonymity of it.

Something bright abided on the floor. A pale rosebud glowed in the faint starlight that filtered through the windows. I bent slowly to retrieve it, half expecting it to dissolve at my touch. It remained silky and real in my cupped hand.

Jane had not used any buds in my bouquet, only fully opened flowers. I stared at the rose for a long time, trying to reason out what it meant.

This was ridiculous. I did not want to be found standing there like a fool, sleepwalking, if some servant happened by. I walked back up to my chambers and bolted myself in, the rosebud still cradled in my hand. I didn't want to let it go. Nothing had seemed so friendly to me in a long time, and I knew I would sleep and wake again to find it had only been a dream.

But the soft scent of the rose lulled me. Made me think of my mother. Long to look on her beauty again, to hear her speak a kind word to me in the gardens. And despite all my efforts, my eyes grew too heavy to hold open, and I fell asleep with the rosebud clutched in my fist.

CHAPTER 9

orning light woke me much later than usual. Neither Jane nor anyone else had disturbed me after the dreams of my strange wedding night.

I stretched, then froze. A white rosebud lay on the bed linens beside me. I lifted it, turning it over in my palm. Brown bruises stained the delicate white petals that I'd clutched the night before. It was the same rosebud. The dancing lights were real.

Did that mean the ghost and the curse were real, too?

I sat up and cradled the rosebud in my hand. The delicate swirl of petals suddenly felt as heavy as gold. The...the ghost had celebrated with me. She—assuming it was Richard's sister—did not object to my presence. She might even welcome it. Was she lonely, then?

I shook my head and pushed my bed curtains aside. Briarwood was making my imagination run wild. I could hear Miss Davidson's stern voice warning me that a young lady ought to give no place to such wild thoughts. No ghosts. Not even novels or fairy stories. She had considered music and drawing only mildly acceptable because they made a young lady useful for entertaining guests. Only practical things like managing the household and needlework warranted much attention.

Well, what could Miss Davidson say against the rosebud? Against the lights that had danced around me the night before? Maybe I could be useful to a lonely ghost.

Yet I knew nothing about Miss Neale except that she had been well-liked and had died tragically in a way that made people suspect her brother. I didn't even know her Christian name.

But she had loved her garden. Hadn't I felt someone there with me on her bench? She had left me a rosebud from that garden. Perhaps she wanted it tended in spite of her brother's objections. I could sneak about when he wasn't home and do a little weeding, at least.

I rang for Jane, who snuck grinning glances at me as she helped me dress.

"You didn't lock the door this time," she noted.

I had not. Feeling that the house—or its ghost—was my ally made me much less afraid even of murderers. Though I did not want to keep Miss Neale company by joining her in haunting the house.

"What else do you need of me today?" Jane asked once my hair was arranged.

"I'm...not certain yet what I will be doing today. We may find ourselves playing cards in the drawing-room, but maybe it won't come to that."

"It's cloudy but not rainy," Jane offered.

"Perhaps I will walk outside." But first, I had to know what my husband was doing.

I went downstairs and found Harris inspecting the ballroom with a frown. Did she notice signs of the night's disturbances?

"Where is my husband this morning?" I asked her.

She gave me a searching look. "Didn't he tell you? He rode out early on some business."

I met her challenging stare. "He allowed me my rest. Do you expect him home for supper?"

Harris looked away. "I never know when to expect him, and if you don't either, then you'll likely be dining alone tonight."

My heart sank at the words in spite of myself. But I should not have been sorry. This was my chance to explore the garden more.

I put on a bonnet and walked outside. The clouds hung low over the terraced gardens, the stone walls cold when I touched them. I glanced at the house, half expecting to see jealous eyes watching me, but the dim light reflecting off the glass made me blind to anyone inside. Better to go first to where I really wanted to explore, then see the rest later.

I hurried to the rose garden. A few blooms clung to the bushes, refusing to acknowledge the coming winter and the rest that awaited them. I wandered among the flowers, taking deep breaths of their sweet perfume and pausing to pull the largest weeds free. A huge dandelion hunkered like a weasel trapped in a corner beneath the thorny branches of a large crimson rose. I crouched and tugged at the dandelion, fighting the roots that had worked their way deep into the soil of Briarwood.

Finally, the weed snapped. I tumbled onto my backside, the breath shocked out of me. I dropped the dandelion leaves and examined several scratches welling with tiny drops of blood on the back of my hand. Heedless of my efforts to help, the rose had slashed me.

I shook my hand. I was going to need a proper pair of leather gloves. Jane could get some from the village so I did not have to ask Richard. It would take many hours to do a proper job of cleaning the garden. Perhaps if I did it in small stages, Richard would not notice, and his sister's spirit would be more at ease.

I saw and felt nothing to alert me that Miss Neale lingered in the garden that day, though. Perhaps she had exhausted herself the night before. Or perhaps even ghosts did not enjoy gloomy days in England.

I wiped my hand clean with a handkerchief and strolled down the terraces to the lake. The heavy, steely sky reflected strangely in the gently rippling waters, like a mirror that did not cast back my reflection. I shivered and pulled my shawl closer around my shoulders. The little grotto on the far side called to me—intriguing, and also a good place to shelter if rain began.

The walk around the lake was quiet, only a few birds calling from the trees, but footprints in the soft ground warned me that I was not the only one who walked this path. Of course, the Briarwood gamekeeper would come this way often for fish, and he would likely stay out of my way if he saw me down here. Or he would spy on me for Richard.

I approached the grotto, admiring the artful arrangement of the stones so that one might pretend it was a natural construct. I peered inside the dusky cave.

A startled face stared back. A strange man.

I gasped and stumbled back, ready to scream.

"Forgive me!" The man cried, showing his empty hands. "I did not mean to startle you."

I backed farther away, glancing over my shoulder in search of the imagined gamekeeper or anyone else who might come to my aid. Had the killer found me so quickly? My throat felt thick. "Who are you? Why are you lurking here?"

"I'm Captain Josiah Reeves. I'm here... I often come because..." He swallowed.

I took a moment to study him. Was he the man from the garden in Bath? The murderer? My stomach curled into a hard lump. I didn't know. How could I be certain? He had a slim build. Perhaps too short. I tried to imagine him in a cloak. A futile effort. Miss Davidson had discouraged me from exercising my imagination, after all. The one way Richard hoped I would help him—being able to identify the mysterious figure—and I was certain to fail at it.

This man's face was dark—not just from the sun, but suggesting some ancestry from a distant land. He did not look angry or scheming as I might expect from a killer stalking me. He appeared only a few years older than me, but his eyes reflected a lifetime's worth of sorrow.

He cleared his throat and went on. "I am mourning, you see. I feel closer to her here."

Miss Neale again. And he's claimed to be a Reeves. A relation of Richard's neighbors. Another person caught in Miss Neale's spell. It had caught me, too, hadn't it? Still, that did not mean I could trust Captain Reeves, or anyone.

"I apologize," he went on. "I did hear that Lord Neale had married. Quietly. Of course, because he's still in mourning. I had not imagined I would intrude."

He had probably thought he could sneak around the estate unhindered the day after a wedding. In fact, it might seem odd that I was out this morning, at least without my husband.

"I am trying to learn more of Briarwood," I said.

"Of course. Since I disrupted your peace, perhaps I could answer questions for you? I spent a great deal of time here these last few years. My father's brother is settled nearby."

"I met the Reeves yesterday," I said.

Captain Reeves nodded. "I am the only offspring of the youngest son of the family. My cousins are in Bath, I believe."

He was either telling the truth about who he was, or he had spied out the situation thoroughly.

"Then it was your aunt and uncle I met yesterday," I said. "Along with the Palmers."

"The triumvirate of the neighborhood's leading families, then, including the Neales." There was a bitter note in his voice. "You will spend a great deal of time in their company, if Lord Neale chooses to be sociable again."

"Will you tell me about...about Miss Neale? I know it is painful for her friends, but few speak of her, and I would like to know her better."

A wistfulness filled his face, and his eyes shone with distant memories. "She was a lovely girl. Kind, good-natured, lively. She had an imagination, always inventing fun if the day was gloomy like this one."

"I understand why so many miss her."

"Yes." Frustration laced his words. "It's why it's so hard to believe... to understand—"

Understand who would have killed a delightful young lady.

"Understand why she's gone," I finished quietly.

He nodded, not able to meet my gaze. I did not know if he was trustworthy, but I believed his grief was real.

"I'm sorry for your loss. Everyone's loss," I said. "I'm sorry I did not have the opportunity to know her."

Captain Reeves nodded stiffly.

"I will leave you to your peace," I said. I turned, then thought of one piece of information Captain Reeves might share that no one at Briarwood was likely to. "It may seem silly, but I wondered if you might tell me... what was her name? None at Briarwood speak it."

He swallowed. "Eleanor." He whispered it like a prayer. "Her name was Eleanor."

CHAPTER 10

Eleanor.

Eleanor Neale.

I now had a name for *her*. For Briarwood's ghost.

But what was I to do with it?

Jane found me as I stood in the entrance to the ballroom, staring without seeing at the high ceilings and wishing the lights would reappear.

"Someday we'll have balls here again," Jane said. "When the period of mourning is over."

I shook myself out of my reverie. "Yes, of course." Though I would not be at Briarwood long enough to see dancing. "Do you know exactly when Miss Neale died? No one has spoken to me of the details."

"I heard it was at a ball after the harvest but before Advent. Apparently, she wished to hold the first event of the winter season to liven up the darker days."

"In November. Not so far away, then." I turned slowly to the ballroom. "Since his sister died at a ball, I doubt Lord Neale will be anxious to hold another one. Too many painful memories."

Jane nodded. "True. I'm certain you could convince him. Only when you feel it's right, of course."

I made a noncommittal noise. I could not even convince Richard to talk to me. "Shall we play cards? Or a table game? I am fond of backgammon if you enjoy it."

It was more a request for a lady's companion than a lady's maid, but Jane would be serving as both in this lonely house.

"Certainly, my lady, if you'll teach me."

We found the drawing room as Lord Neale had promised, well stocked with ways to entertain ourselves. A less dreary prison than some. I did enjoy backgammon and had played to distract my brother or my father at times. Miss Davidson had sneered at it as a waste of time, but acceptable if I was doing it to keep the men in my family entertained. Just as music was a barely acceptable pastime. I had learned to play but never found much joy in it. It was just another chore, like inspecting the silver or stitching a pillow cover.

Jane hadn't played many games, having been raised to the work of a maid, but she learned quickly, and it wasn't long before we were able to challenge each other.

Voices in the main corridor broke our quiet concentration. My breath quickened. Was that Richard?

"Just a moment," I told Jane and went out to look.

Richard stood in the entrance hall with his valet Walters, both dressed in clothes still dusty from riding.

"You are returned!" I stepped forward, away of Walters watching, along with the house's many carved and painted eyes. "You'll be joining me for supper, then?"

Richard hesitated, and my chest tightened. He did not wish to spend time with me. My conversation was not as interesting as he'd expected, then, and I had nothing else to offer him. He did not give me a chance!

Walters politely averted his gaze from the exchange. He was a sparse man with sparse hair, approaching middle age, and I wondered if he enjoyed his young master's nighttime adventures or if he was only very loyal and desirous to indulge or protect him.

"We will not be here for supper." Richard didn't meet my eyes. "Don't expect to see me often."

Disappointment lanced through me, an almost-physical blow to my chest.

"You are going out again so late?" I asked quietly. Then realization dawned. "Ah."

"Yes, as you say," Richard replied. "I am about my business. You needn't concern yourself. In fact, the less you're involved, the better."

"Isn't it too late for that?" I asked. "The only reason I'm here—"

"You are here because Briarwood needed a lady," he said with a warning in his voice. "My activities keep you safe."

"Yes," I said. Did he really think the murderer was lurking in his own house, that he had to dissemble in front of his valet-turned-henchman?

"Good night," he said with finality.

I didn't respond to the abrupt dismissal, just turned

and headed back for the drawing-room. I didn't see how him robbing innocent travelers would keep me safe. If anything, it put me in more danger. If he was caught or killed, I was even more ruined than before. Not only would it make me a social pariah all over again, but if the killer had connected me to the highwayman, it would reveal me and leave me without protection.

With those cheerful thoughts darkening my mind, Jane trounced me at backgammon and then at cards, and I had little appetite for supper.

When night came, I could not fall asleep. Night's stillness gathering in my chambers, but the darkness fed the gloom gnawing on my mind.

Well, what was keeping me in my rooms? Richard was out, and so was his valet. Harris had to sleep sometime. At night, Briarwood could be mine.

I threw on my dressing gown and slipped into the corridor, searching for Eleanor.

The house was dark, lit only by a half moon that peeked through tall, narrow windows. The corridors were eerily empty with all the servants asleep for the night. I had the entirety of Briarwood to myself, yet I did not feel alone. It sent shivers over my skin, the sense that someone walked near me. Eleanor, perhaps? I almost spoke to her but felt silly for the impulse. What if she didn't respond?

What if she did?

I hesitated before entering Richard's wing of the house, my pulse thrumming in my ears. Down the corridor, a light shone. Richard and his valet were out. Had someone left a candle burning? That was dangerous. I hurried forward, and the light retreated before me.

I stopped, the hairs on my head prickling. The light stopped, too. Like someone was leading me onward, though I heard no footsteps and saw no shadows. Only the glow of a light just out of reach.

I swallowed and summoned my courage.

"Eleanor, is that you?"

Nothing, though the light might have bobbed a little, like it was impatient for me to follow. I stood very still in the corridor. Somewhere, a clock ticked, the only sound in the house, like a hushed heartbeat. Following a ghost was definitely *not* practical.

Yet this might be my chance to be useful to someone—to someone I believed was being kind to me in her way.

I let out a slow breath and followed the glowing orb.

The light led me to a room partway down the corridor. It vanished through the door. I assumed it would be locked, but when I tried the handle, the door swung open.

I stepped inside, expecting darkness, but moonlight flooded the room. I gasped. It was a library. Nothing like my father's library, which was a single bookshelf next to his desk with a few dusty religious and agricultural tracts. These walls each held two tall, wide bookshelves like stocky footmen standing at attention. The shelves sheltered a wealth of books. Beautiful volumes bound in red, brown, or black leather, the titles written in gold leaf. I quickly scanned the titles. Shakespeare, Milton, Pope. There were even novels. Forbidden delights. But Miss Davidson was no longer here to tell me I must not waste my mind on them.

No one cared what I wasted my mind on now.

I ran my fingers over the soft leather of the well-worn spines. Was this what Eleanor wanted to share with me? A little dust rose to tickle my nose, but not enough to suggest the room had been utterly forsaken. I didn't feel right about taking the books back to my chambers, so I would have to read them here in this forgotten room. A writing table stood near the fireplace, close enough to be comfortable on a chilly day, but protected from the glare and smoke by a screen. No, that was someone's personal space. The chair by the window —that was where I would read. But what would I start with? I had seen snippets of Shakespeare performed and thought his language was lovely. But the novels called to me. The thing most forbidden was the one I desired the most.

I touched the faint indentation of the gold title on *Evelina, Vol I*. It felt a little sacrilegious, like I was caressing the statues of a saint in a church. I gently eased the book from its place.

A movement from the window caught my eye. I gasped and pushed the novel back into its place, pressing my hand to my racing heart. A figure strode through the moonlight.

Richard. He had returned safely. I wondered if he had found whatever answers he sought out there on the highways under the stars.

I did not think he had seen me. In fact, I was certain he had not or he would have come to give me a tongue-lashing. I glanced regretfully at *Evelina* then hurried out of the library and back to my wing of the house, my pulse pounding in my ears. Once my heartbeat had calmed, I considered the rows of lovely books sitting silent and neglected, waiting to be loved again.

"I will return," I promised the dark corridor.

I thought that Eleanor understood.

CHAPTER II

I faced many days of quiet, playing games, embroidering linens, or pressing flowers with Jane, even plinking out some cotillions and minuets on the piano-forte. Other than attending church on Sundays, I rarely ventured out, and even at church, we sat alone and apart. I glimpsed the upright Reeves and the gray-haired Palmers, but I knew no one else, and no one dared speak to the cursed Neales, even in the sanctuary of the church.

At night, when I saw and heard no sign of my husband, I snuck to his wing of the house and familiarized myself with the library. I was a starved person who had discovered bread. The Gothic novels especially gave me pleasant shivers as I bent over them. Fanny Burney, Ann Radcliffe, and Samuel Richardson swept me away to unimagined places and gave me a new perspective on familiar ones. I saw no more sign of Eleanor, but I felt her, as if she were reading over my shoulder.

But the peace could not last. Harris found Jane and me at our cards one afternoon, her expression troubled. Had she discovered my clandestine activities? My stomach fluttered uneasily.

"Do you need something, Harris?" I asked, keeping my voice level.

"The Reeves have come to call." She hesitated, as if about to announce the roof was leaking. "And that silly French girl."

I didn't know any silly French girl, but Richard was concerned about anyone prying into our arrangement or our life. "We did expect the Reeves to call at some time."

Harris made a noncommittal sound.

"Were they not common visitors...before?" I asked.

"Miss Louisa Reeves came sometimes, but I haven't seen her, since..." Harris shrugged helplessly.

I nodded. "See them into the blue drawing room and bring tea. I'll be right along."

Jane watched me closely, no doubt seeing my uneasiness even if she did not know the cause. "You'll do fine, my lady. If they don't love you, it's because they're not worth knowing."

I gave her a wan smile and stood to straighten my gowns. Jane helped me with some stray hairs, and then I was ready for my role as Lady Neale, who had nothing to hide from her neighbors or anyone else.

Our guests—one young man and three young women—stood when I entered the room and greeted me with curtseys and bows. The first woman was a strutting creature who looked ready to take charge of every room she entered, the top chicken in the henhouse. She reminded me of Frances, but I needed to give her a fair chance. She was shadowed by a frail-looking girl with big, sad eyes, who stared around the room like she expected someone to jump out from one of the corners.

I recognized the French girl from Bath: Mademoiselle de Carriere. She was almost as pretty as Eleanor's roses, with her brown curls and bright blue eyes. How interesting that she was here with the Reeves. Perhaps they had been at that ball, too, but of course I didn't know them then and wouldn't have remembered them among so many faces. I only hoped that they would not connect me to the body in the garden and send out rumors that would lead the killer to me.

The young man raised a lazy hand to straighten his collar, barely bothering to regard me at all. Good. Let him overlook me.

The commanding little woman stepped forward and looked me over with a not-altogether-pleased air.

"So, you are Lady Neale. I am Miss Mary Reeves, and this is my sister, Miss Louisa, my brother, Mr. John Reeves, and our guest, Mademoiselle de Carriere."

They all expressed some degree of congratulations for my marriage, Mademoiselle Carriere with the most convincing sincerity in her softly accented English.

"I am glad to meet you all," I said, especially meeting Miss Louisa's eyes. From Harris's words, I surmised she had been a friend of Eleanor. They all continued staring at me, so I added, "Please, be seated."

Mary sat on the edge of one of the chairs and looked around the room. "I'm glad to see this place hasn't gone to rack and ruin as some people said."

"Oh?" I raised my eyebrows.

"Mary!" John snapped at his sister. He looked at me. "Forgive my sister. Her tongue often runs away with her."

Mary glared back at him. "*I* wasn't the one who said it. I'm only saying that *some* have expressed their suspicions about the state of things here. Now we will be able to tell everyone otherwise." She sniffed. "Much different from the Palmers. They maintain an air of respectability, but I heard ladies in Bath saying she's made over the same gowns for six or seven seasons!"

"That's economical of her," I said. As Father sank to his lowest, I made over many an old gown. If I did become Mrs. Palmer's lady's companion after this marriage ended, my practical skills would be useful to her.

"Oh, economical, yes." Mary tittered. "But a little sad, don't you think?"

I smiled stiffly. She must not yet have connected me to my father's scandal. Or she had, and she was baiting me. I curled my fingers into the soft velvet of the chair cushion.

The arrival of tea provided relief from the awkwardness —but only for a moment.

Louisa took her cup and stared down at it, tears forming in her eyes.

"Louisa," Mary hissed loudly enough for any eavesdropping servants to hear. "You said you could maintain your composure."

Louisa set her cup down with trembling hands. "I thought... I miss her, and it's the first time returning."

Mary and John rolled their eyes, but Mademoiselle Carriere placed a gentle hand over Louisa's.

I let out a slow breath. This was like walking across a cow field: I was almost certain to end up stepping in something unpleasant.

"I'm sorry I never had the chance to meet Miss Neale," I said. "She was obviously well-loved to be mourned so deeply."

"She was the sweetest, brightest friend one could ever have," Louisa declared between sniffles.

"Yes, she is widely missed," John put in quickly. "Such a shame she met an untimely end. I suppose we cannot get to know each other without the topic coming up, though I'm afraid you'll find the general population has moved past mourning."

"We need a fresh topic for conversation," Mary declared.

Louisa glared at her.

"I'm afraid for me it *is* a fresh topic," I said, "but I can understand it might not be pleasant for those who have heard so much of it." I glanced at the siblings. "Perhaps Miss Louisa and I can talk about it some other time."

Louisa gave me a watery smile and dabbed her nose again.

"You must feel absolutely bereft here," Mary said. "With your husband still in mourning and you not able to enjoy yourself. We'll tell you all about Bath."

And so began a deluge of gossip. I needed an umbrella to stop all the Miss So-and-sos and Mister This-and-that's Mary poured over my head.

"And the highwayman becomes bolder!" Mary leaned forward, her eyes bright in the throes of gossip—not a pleasant brightness, but more of the look of one caught in a fever.

"The...the highwayman?" My voice caught. I wasn't sure how much I was supposed to know about the highwayman, but I was certainly interested in my husband's welfare.

"They'll catch him soon enough," John said, studying his nails with a sneer of disinterest.

"He does seem reckless," Mary said.

"I hope they do not catch him!" Louisa clutched her soggy handkerchief. "He's like someone out of Eleanor's stories."

"Her stories?" I asked.

Louisa's eyes brightened. "Oh, yes! Surely, you've seen them. She has...*had* such a wonderful library full of stories."

"Ah." I wasn't supposed to know about her books. I couldn't be sure Harris or another servant wasn't lurking within earshot, ready to report to Richard that I had been prying. "We...don't use the library."

"Really?" Mary's eyebrows reared up like excited caterpillars. "Whyever not?"

"Um..." I scrambled for a harmless lie. Briarwood's many eyes watched, waiting. Carved faces that Eleanor had somehow appreciated. An idea struck. "Richard wanted the library preserved untouched out of respect for his sister."

"How Gothic of him." Mary's lips curled into an unpleasant smile.

My stomach knotted. Somehow, she would twist my response into unpleasant gossip.

"I think it's romantic." Louisa sighed. "Though I wonder if she would have wanted her books untouched... I know she would have liked to hear about the highwayman. He's romantic, too."

John laughed. "Are you in love with him like everyone else? Silly girl, nothing in life is like your stories. He's just a criminal, and he will end at the gallows like one."

My fingers turned cold despite the heat rising from my tea. They didn't hang lords, but they could certainly execute him. I set my cup down on its saucer a little unsteadily, the tink of china against china loud to my ears.

"Oh, pardon me," Richard's cool voice came from the doorway. "I heard the voices."

I gave a start, and my cheeks warmed as if I'd been caught misbehaving.

John smirked. "The Reeves have come to congratulate you on your marriage, my lord. But never fear, we did not bring our cousin."

Mary snickered quietly at that, and Richard's expression darkened.

I tried to keep my face neutral. My husband did not care for Captain Reeves, then? Did he suspect him of harming Eleanor?

"We have intruded on Lady Neale's time long enough, sisters," John said.

Richard gave him a small bow and stood waiting while the ladies gathered their fans and handkerchiefs and scurried away. Louisa cast a glance back at me, and I knew I would see her again. Of all the siblings, she was the most tolerable—she and Mademoiselle Carriere.

Once they were gone, Richard turned to me. "I apologize for leaving you to face them alone."

"I'm glad to have been of service. It is a lady's duty."

"Not the most pleasant one," Richard said sympathetically.

I couldn't help a chuckle. "They were rather awful—Mary in particular. I suppose she must find life here very dull to thrive so on gossip."

Richard smiled a little. "Do you often make excuses for people's poor manners? My sister…" His smile faded, but there was still a glimmer of it in his eyes. "She often speculated that Mary Reeves must have suffered a Grave Disappointment to always look at things in such a negative light."

Richard had never spoken so openly of his sister.

I stepped closer, measuring my response carefully. "I begin to understand why she was so loved."

Richard swallowed and nodded. He glanced toward the entrance hall. "At least the Reeves will likely not trouble you often. Briarwood might provide them with gossip, but no more entertainment than that."

That gave me an opening. "Who is this cousin they mentioned?"

Richard's hand twitched into a fist. "A trouble maker. He will never show his face here again, so you need not—"

"Concern myself with him." I met his eyes. "Yes, I know. But I must have *something* to concern myself with."

"You are tired of cards and games."

"Yes."

He looked thoughtful. "I suppose you will be expected to return the call."

"Miss Louisa would not be so bad to speak with again," I said.

"You may be polite, for appearance's sake, but remember to be cautious with all of the Reeves."

"I can hardly imagine Miss Louisa harming anyone... Oh, but her sister is a terrible gossip."

"Yes. You see the problem." His voice softened. "I am sorry to force you to remain isolated, but it's not safe."

"Perhaps, then, you will have supper with me?" I asked, my breath fluttering in my chest, where I held it.

He looked torn for a moment, but then his unreadable mask fell back into place. "No, I'd best not. I will be going out again soon."

My shoulders sagged. He bowed and left me more alone than ever.

CHAPTER 12

Since Richard rode the highways again—becoming bolder, the Reeves had said—I took advantage of the opportunity to weed the garden. I yanked up weed after weed, leaving a trail of destruction behind me like a floral Robespierre, not caring if Richard noticed. It filled my chest with a savage pleasure. And once the house had gone to sleep, I snuck back to the library.

I selected a book from the shelves and looked around the room, planning to settle into my usual chair. A faint glow arose above the desk, an invitation to look. I had mostly ignored the desk thus far, feeling I ought not invade someone else's private space.

As I hesitated, the fold-up wooden writing surface that concealed the desk's interior dropped open with a snap. I jumped and clutched the book to my chest, staring at the newly-revealed papers and compartments. Then I chuckled nervously.

"You want me to see," I whispered to Eleanor. Certainly, her brother would have already looked for clues in the desk. Or perhaps not, given how everyone avoided everything to do with Eleanor. "Very well."

I slid into the delicate wooden chair at the desk. It was a strange feeling, sharing space with a dead woman. Like I knew her and yet did not. It wasn't that she was forgotten. Her absence was a constant pressure, like a drain had been pulled in a tub and everything circled it, spiraling down. And that was the problem. She wanted the drain stoppered and the water to be still again. I didn't know how I knew that. Miss Davidson would have said reading was deranging my weak senses. But I felt Eleanor's presence, a warmth over my shoulder, whispering to me.

She wanted me to search the documents. I could almost hear the words. I shifted the papers closer and wrinkled my nose at the dust that stirred. Everything was jumbled together. Letters from her brother and from friends in London. Some typical-looking legal documents. Images torn from fashion magazines.

But beneath that top layer were stories. Handwriting covered the pages, delicate loops filling the space and excited tittles dancing above each "i." I lifted the smooth, cream-colored papers reverently and spread them on the desk.

I skimmed the contents. The first was about a knight and a lady, brother and sister, and their adventures fighting monsters and rescuing their kingdom. They were light-hearted, almost childish, but I enjoyed reading them. It did not take me long to recognize Richard as the knight. The lady in the story was Eleanor, then.

She showed me a Richard I had never known. One who laughed and spoke freely. Perhaps, a Richard not in mourning. I wished I could have known that Richard. He sounded like a good brother—a good friend. An ache bloomed in my chest for what was lost.

The next story was about a noble highwayman... Oh, dear. Was this where Richard encountered the idea of becoming a highwayman? Was he living out his sister's stories? Or had he been a highwayman before, and his sister was writing about it then? No, I believed he only started after her death.

"Were these the stories Miss Louisa mentioned?" I whispered in case Eleanor could hear. Not just books, but her own tales. Did she know her brother was playing the highwayman now, inspired by her writings? Did she disapprove?

As I read on, the tone of her stories changed, darkened. Some stories were as dramatic as the library's Gothic novels. Secret identities. Missing people. Threats of murder. In these stories, I could not always identify the inspiration for the protagonists, if there were any. But one tale included a cousin from a distant land, wrongfully scorned by his family. Several featured an inveterate gossip who annoyed everyone by saying rude things followed by, "I'm only repeating what others say." The Reeves.

I sat back and blinked at the candle flickering low in its silver candlestick. Richard was not really a knight, but if there was any truth to Eleanor's stories, what of the tales of secret identities and threatened murder?

I stood and paced to the window, trying to clear my head.

A figure stood below the window. I froze.

It was Richard. He had not seen me. He stood in front of the house and let the moonlight pour over him. His head was bowed, his usually upright posture slack, as though he was overcome with powerful fatigue. I touched the cool glass, wishing again that he would let me help him.

He rubbed his eyes and turned in my direction. His gaze met mine. A jolt raced through me. I needed to retreat to my chamber. No, that was ridiculous. He had seen me.

He glowered and stormed toward the house. I winced and awaited my fate, my pulse pounding in my throat. I gently closed the desk and stepped away from it again. Eleanor had welcomed me to look, but Richard wouldn't understand.

It took only a minute or two before the door burst open. The candle guttered at the sudden draft.

"What are you doing in my sister's library?" Richard asked.

I stepped back, my throat tight, but forced myself to meet his accusing gaze. "I thought I saw a light."

He watched me with narrowed eyes, all the tension returned to his posture. "A light?"

"Yes." I swallowed. "In the corridor. Coming from in here. I wondered what it was."

"I told you not to come into this wing of the house."

"I know. But...the light made me curious."

He continued to frown, but I had the sense he wasn't frowning at me anymore. Instead, he was seeing some distant memory.

Before he could order me out, I blurted, "May I read the books?"

He blinked slowly and looked around the room, as though just realizing it was full of expensive volumes. "You like to read?"

"I do." My voice came out in a strangled whisper. "My father...my governess...did not allow me to read for pleasure. But I would like to. To pass the time."

My heart beat hard in the silence.

He stared at me, his expression impossible to read in the moonlight. "You never read books for enjoyment?"

I shook my head, not trusting my voice to stay steady. I had never had the opportunity before Briarwood. I silently prayed he would not take the pleasure away from me now. He could not lock a garden, but he could lock a library.

He walked past me and made a slow circuit of the room, staring at each of the shelves in turn. I clasped my hands together, imagining all the stories he might deny me. My fingers felt icy.

Then he faced me again. "My sister loved to read."

"She had a great many books," I said cautiously.

"Yes. I bought many of them for her. My father bought the others. I used to read some of them with her. Now, no one reads them."

"That seems a shame," I said and instantly wondered if it was the wrong thing. After all, Richard wouldn't let me anywhere near the gardens, no matter if his sister would have wanted them cared for.

But Richard sighed. "It does. She would not have liked it," he said more to himself than to me. Then he looked up, his dark eyes fastened on mine. "Very well. You may read her books. But you are to stay out of this room. I will deliver books to the drawing room for you to read."

I didn't think that was what Eleanor wanted. She wanted me to see her stories. But this was a start, and Richard was treating me with more consideration than I would have expected given that I had broken his rules and intruded on his privacy. He behaved more like the knight of Eleanor's stories than the cold lord he portrayed for the world at large. Maybe Eleanor's Richard was not entirely gone. The chill inside me lifted.

"Thank you," I said, stepping toward him.

He shrugged off the gratitude and turned from me. "Now, return to your wing."

CHAPTER 13

Richard brought me books, as promised, and I welcomed their company—new adventures and friends wrapped in the scent of leather and ink. I still itched to return to the library and the desk, but I didn't dare. Eleanor wanted me there, but Richard did not, and he could lock me out if he wished.

One evening, I read late in the drawing room, having sent Jane to bed so I could discover if Emily would ever escape Udolpho and find love with Valancourt. A noise in the stairway almost made me drop my book. My mind full of ghosts and secret passages, I hurried out to see if Eleanor was haunting the corridors. Instead, I stumbled into Richard. He was dressed in his highwayman costume, the hat pulled low and the mask over his face so I could only see his dark eyes behind the eerie white mask. I hesitated, my heart beating hard, though I knew the mask and the man behind it were no threat to me.

He quickly pulled the mask off and made a small bow.

"You are riding out tonight," I said, trying not to sound disappointed.

"As you see."

I thought of his sister's stories of him, how he laughed and played the part of a heroic rescuer. I did not think she would like him being a real highwayman, even a dashing one. The stories were safe, but things that were secure and simple in stories were not so in real life.

"I wish you would not," I said quietly.

His eyes fixed on me. "Whyever not?"

"It's dangerous. Someday, someone may defend themselves, you know."

"Then you would be a widow with a fine house all to yourself."

My stomach lurched at the thought. "Maybe I don't want to always be alone."

Neale stared at me, his expression impossible to read. "Are you truly so very lonely here?"

"Of course," I said. "There's no one here but you and the servants, and Jane is the only one who speaks to me. If it weren't for her and the books, I think I would go mad."

We stared at each other in the dimness. Sympathy flickered in Richard's eyes, and I impulsively reached out for him, wishing he would show me the Richard who could laugh with me or even the highwayman who had complemented me and kissed my hand.

He took my fingers, and my heart gave a leap.

But he only bowed over my hand and released it. "Thank

goodness for Jane and the books, then! We cannot have you losing your mind. One madman is quite enough for this household."

With that, he turned to leave.

"Must you leave?" I asked quietly, hating the pleading in my voice.

"I must." His voice was resolute, and he did not meet my eyes.

"Why? You don't need the wealth. What are you searching for?"

"Answers," he said.

"Let me help! It would give me something to do. Some way to be useful."

Now he did glance at me. "Why do you always want to be useful?"

"Because...because what value is a person who is not useful?"

He looked perplexed behind the mask. "You think your value lies in what you accomplish?"

"I..." Did I believe that? "I suppose so."

He looked down at the grotesque mask in his hands. "Well, my value lies in finding my answers. My penance is in the search. No one else can do it for me."

And with that, he walked out into the night.

I bit back a scream of frustration. Answers! I needed answers, too, and he was not inclined to give them to me. I thought perhaps his sister was trying to help, but I did not understand the answers she provided.

I raced up the stairs to the library and flung the desk

open. Eleanor's stories waited there. She had written about her friends and neighbors. About secrets and danger. Was there a clue in these pages that would lead me to her murderer?

"What do you want me to find?" I asked.

A faint light rose around the desk, but it did not tell me what I was looking for. I thumbed through more of the stories. One was a variation on Red Riding Hood where the wolf appeared at first as a kind gentleman whose predatory traits slowly unfolded as his disguise fell apart—first his ears, then his eyes, and then his teeth. And he gobbled Red Riding Hood up. I shivered and set the pages down.

"Did you know he was coming for you, then?" I asked the stillness of the dark. "Who was your wolf?"

But in death, Eleanor had no voice. Only the words she had left behind.

Helpless. Voiceless. I felt a kinship with her. Suddenly too weary to keep reading, I went to bed.

I didn't see Richard the next morning, though I supposed that someone would bring me news if he had been shot down on the road as a common highwayman. I was too restless to sit in the drawing-room, especially on a fine day. I sent Jane off on some errands and worked a little in the garden, but even that did not satisfy my itch to move. I rose with a huff and wandered the grounds.

As I neared the pond, I once again spotted Captain Reeves. Having met the rest of his family, I was curious to know him better. He was especially unwelcome at Briarwood. Given his obvious interest in Eleanor, I suspected that was the cause of the rift. But did that mean Richard suspected Captain Reeves of killing of Eleanor? Of murdering the man in the garden in Bath? As I watched Captain Reeves stride along the edge of the pond, I tried to picture him as the cloaked man I'd seen in the garden. It was possible, but that could be true of almost anyone.

"Good morrow," he called.

"Good morrow. I am sorry to disturb your wanderings."

He smiled. "But I am the one intruding. I have to admit I have little enjoyment of being at my family's home."

"I understand," I said.

He gave me a curious look.

"Your cousins came to call on me."

He chuckled. "I see. The problems of polite society."

"You don't join them on social occasions?"

He looked away, his eyes on the faint ripples of the water. "I'm rarely invited. You see, my father was a bit of a black sheep. He ran off to India and made his fortune there, as well as marrying my mother, who was East Indian."

"And that's why the Reeves don't treat you kindly? How dreadful of them!"

He grinned. "Well, they don't like the reminder that their fields produce wild grains."

"Your father, you mean?"

"In fact, the current Mr. Reeves was the only respectable sibling—the only one to uphold the legacy of a proper Saxon squire. The older brother—the original heir—ran off to the continent after killing someone in a duel and is said to have ended a dissolute life abroad. And there was a sister who became a royal mistress."

My eyes widened. "But they're so... so—"

"Yes, they are," he said with a twinkle in his eye. "And now you know why. They are desperate to make people forget their scandalous connections."

I thought of Mary Reeves and her addiction to gossip. Was this how she came to it—distracting attention from her own family's stained linens by pointing out everyone else's?

"Well, I've endured my own share of gossip." I bit my tongue. I should not have given him any clue to who I was. He was pleasant to talk to, but Eleanor's wolf must have been as well—before his canine features showed.

"I'm sorry to hear it. I've learned to give little regard to what people think of me."

I tried to do the same, but it was not easy. "Do you plan to return to sea?"

He looked confused for a moment, then he chuckled. "I wasn't a sea captain—I was a captain in the East India Company's army." His smile faded. "And no, I never again want to be a part of the atrocities taking place there."

"I'm sorry." I fell silent, not certain what to say. But then I thought of Eleanor's garden. "You must be the one who brought Eleanor her roses! I have never seen such flowers."

"I wish I could claim credit for that, because she loved them. But no, she had them already when I came here from India. They were the thing that first drew us into conversation." He smiled wistfully.

"I won't chase you away from the gardens if you wish to stroll there."

"That is kind of you, though I'm afraid this is as close as I can come to Briarwood. Lord Neale does not welcome my company."

"I'm not sure he welcomes anyone's company," I said, a trace of bitterness in my voice.

"He was not always thus. He is mourning still."

I gave the captain a sharp look at his own sad tone, but he was staring off into the distance.

"I see," I said. "Well, we should not expect mourning to end when one puts off their black."

He smiled sadly. "No, not when the love was real."

What must that kind of love be like? But I would not ask the captain that question. "Tell me about Lord Neale. What was he like…before?"

"Oh, you must not think he was much different. He has always been reserved. He and his sister were very different that way."

"They were close," I said.

"Yes. He was always protective of her, but she was the one who could coax him out of his seriousness. He inherited his position young, and I think it weighs heavily on him."

"Of course." The protective brother who could not protect his sister at the end. If he was already serious, it would be an even more terrible burden. "You know he did not kill her."

"Yes. Nor did I, despite what some people think."

I raised an eyebrow.

"It was no secret that I loved her, or that her brother did not approve."

"Because of your mother?" I asked.

"No, I give him more credit than that. I don't think he objected to me personally. No one would have been good enough for his sister. And she hated to cause trouble with him, so we didn't press the point. We were both young. We thought we had time…"

"I'm sorry," I murmured, and stood in silence with him for a time.

He might have a reason to kill her if he wanted to marry and she refused to pick him over her brother's objections, but I doubted Captain Reeves had harmed her.

"Who could have hurt someone so universally beloved?" I whispered, as much to myself as to the captain.

He shook his head. "I wish I knew. I would… I don't know what I would do to them. I would beg them to undo it if I could." He stared up at the gardens. "It happened there, you know. In her garden."

A chill raced over me, followed by a sick sensation. "In her garden?"

No wonder Richard did not want me or anyone else there!

Captain Reeves nodded, his face pale. "During the ball. There were so many people—visitors from Bath and from our neighborhood. It seems hard to imagine that a common thief would have been so bold as to attack during a party with so many people present."

"So, it must have been one of…" One of us. A member of Society.

"Probably. One of the people who walks through ballrooms and drawing-rooms, bowing and smiling politely. Hiding evil behind their politeness. That is why I no longer care much for Society or what it thinks of me. There are too many… too many…"

"Wolves," I whispered.

"Indeed. Many wolves in the flock—perhaps more wolves than sheep."

"Yes," I said, my voice tight.

And Richard had taken it upon himself to hunt them.

CHAPTER 14

I returned to the gardens after my conversation with Captain Reeves, walking through them slowly. Someone had murdered Eleanor here, among her beloved roses. Had they followed her from the ball? Lured her outside? She must have realized too late the wolf had cornered her. Did she fight back?

Recalling the pearl I'd found among the weeds, I knelt and searched the ground, carefully turning over the top layer of soil. Now that I was looking, I found two more pearls. Pearls ripped from her as she defended herself, or as she lay dying, help coming too late.

I sat heavily on Eleanor's cold bench, gently rubbing the pearls clean. Beneath the dirt, they still had their faint luster. The wolf had not taken that away. They had been waiting for someone to find them and restore them. Eleanor had been waiting. I rolled them in my palm, marveling at their almost perfect smoothness, and I waited for Richard to find me.

As I expected, he bore down on me from the stables, his expression stormy.

"I told you—" he boomed.

I closed my fist around Eleanor's pearls and lifted my chin. "What are you searching for?"

"What?" he asked, thrown off by my direct approach.

"You're looking for something when you ride the roads— something specific. You searched our jewelry very carefully. Do you know something the killer was wearing when he struck, or did he take something of your sister's?"

He stared me down in silence.

Finally, I held out the pearls. "These were hers. Did the killer steal the rest of them?"

He looked at them for a long moment, then slowly took them from my open hand, his fingers grazing my palm. Sparks flared over my skin at the light contact.

"Yes," he said softly. "He took her jewelry. These came from the necklace she wore that night."

"Perhaps, then, a thief..."

"No. I considered it, but it isn't logical. The house was full of people. Full of the *beau-monde*. No common thief would think it worth the risk to rob a girl in such circum- stances. And much of what he took wasn't as valuable in monetary terms as in sentimental ones. She was very senti- mental." He shook his head. "And I've heard rumors. The man who was killed in the garden that night in Bath...he mentioned an acquaintance who bragged about gaining wealth from Briarwood. What could the killer mean but something he stole from her?"

"So, you are robbing people as a pretense to search their jewels."

He didn't confirm it, but the tightening of his mouth betrayed him.

"Why would he keep the jewels?" I asked, half to myself.

Richard sighed and sat next to me on the bench. I sat rigid for a moment, then relaxed into the companionable feeling, letting my knee brush against his. Warm washed over me despite the late autumn chill in the garden.

"The jewelry is one of the only clues I have," he said, his voice low, "and I ask myself about it often. My first guess was that he killed her in a fit of passion, and he kept the jewels to remember her. If he sold them, I might find them and trace them back to him—and I have checked every jeweler and pawn-shop in England. So, he's keeping them either to remember her or to hide his crime. Either way, he would hold them close."

I considered that. If Richard knew about Captain Reeves's infatuation with his sister, no wonder he suspected him. I doubted that Captain Reeves killed Eleanor, but I did not know him well enough to rule out an accident committed in a fit of rage. Did Eleanor have other suitors? Or was there another reason a killer would keep something from his victims?

"I wonder..." I said.

"Yes?" Richard asked warily.

"I remembered a classmate of Julian's who came to hunt at our estate. He wasn't welcome many other places. There was something disquieting about him..." I shuddered. "One of the things that made my hackles rise was an odd habit he had. After he killed an animal, he would keep some piece of it for his collection. The tails of foxes, tail feathers from birds. It seemed to be a way of tracking his conquests."

Richard went very still at my words. I braced myself, afraid of what pain I must have caused him with this new idea.

He let out a long breath. "Yes, there are predators that prowl among Society."

"Wolves," I said. "But I begin to believe that's unfair, my lord."

He looked at me in surprise.

I wet my lips, and his gaze drifted down to them for a moment.

I flushed and stared at my hands in my lap. "Wolves, from what I understand, hunt because they must, not because they enjoy it and want to remember it."

Richard's lips curled back. "This is why you must not involve yourself in my quest."

"This is why I must! Remember, this man is also hunting me. How can you expect me to sit still and do nothing while some killer stalks closer?"

"I suppose you cannot trust me to keep you safe." His words were so bitter, it sent a shock through me.

"My lord. Richard."

He looked at me in surprise when I used his Christian name.

I cautiously laid my hand over his, my skin warming at my boldness. "I would not have come here if I didn't trust you. I think I'm safer here than anywhere else. But if we're dealing with such a dangerous person, we should be allies. I'm not useless."

"No, of course you're not..."

I laughed humorlessly. "But I am, at least at Briarwood. What have I been doing except sitting here hoping someone will come try to kill me so you can catch them?"

He looked thoughtful. "I can see why that would be uncomfortable for you. I'm surprised you have trusted me as much as you have."

"I wish you would trust me as well. Let me work with you!"

"You cannot ride the highways."

"But there must be something I can do."

He looked down at our overlapping hands, his face softening. A flutter of hope stirred in my chest.

Then he drew a sharp breath. "No. Your first duty is to stay safe, and I will make certain that happens."

With that, he stood and left me. I wrapped my arms around myself, shivering at the chill.

CHAPTER 15

Richard rode the highways again that night, and I was left to sulk in the house. Staying safe, he would say. But it didn't feel safe to sit doing nothing, waiting on others. Worrying about him.

As long as I was trapped inside, alone, I could at least see what else hid in Eleanor's library. Richard didn't want me there, but she did, and he didn't know or care what I did while he was gone.

Once the house had settled into its nighttime quiet, I pulled on my dressing gown and took a candle. The thin light from the moon cast an eerie glow in the dark corridor. The portraits and carved faces watched me from long shadows, their eyes bright in the flickering candlelight as I snuck past them.

As soon as I passed into the family's wing of the house, tiny, ghostly globes of light gathered around me.

"Yes, I'm coming to your library," I whispered.

The lights swirled overhead like agitated birds, then whirled in front of me, forming a glimmering barrier in the rough shape of a person.

I stopped, my chest tightening. "You wish me to stay away from your library?"

The lights bobbed as if each was trying to nod, making the figure ripple. I shivered and looked past the eerie form to the dark corridor beyond.

"Is there somewhere else I ought to go?"

The lights swirled like a glowing waterspout. Some of them brushed me as if trying to take my arm, but I felt nothing as the sparkles passed over my skin.

"If you can't communicate, you will have to guide me."

The lights whisked up overhead and blinked out.

"Well, I can't go up there."

I tiptoed forward, waiting for Eleanor's lights to show me the way.

A thump echoed down the corridor, and I froze. Was Richard home? Maybe he'd found something on his night-time ride. I crept over the plush carpet, approaching the library.

Something moved. A shadow in the darkened doorway of the library. I froze. Richard would not be creeping about his home in the dark, and none of the servants had reason to be in the library at night.

I blew out the candle. My hands turned clammy, and I clutched the candlestick to my chest against the thudding of my heart.

I crept backward. The floorboards creaked underfoot.

The shadow in the library froze.

I paused as well. Should I scream for the servants? Run and hope no one followed?

The figure strode out of the library, cloak billowing around him. I knew that form. That air of menace. It was the killer from Bath.

"Get back!" I rasped, my mouth dry, my words caught in my throat.

I hurled my candlestick at the man. He ducked aside, and the brass clattered to the floor. I scrambled back, looking for something to defend myself. The portraits on the wall watched me with indifference. I picked up a vase from a side table and prepared to lob it at the intruder's head.

Eleanor's lights surged to life, buzzing like a swarm of hornets toward the intruder. He whirled and blocked his face. I lunged forward and smashed the vase over his head.

He growled in fury and slammed my face with a back-handed blow.

Spots exploded across my vision—not Eleanor, but dark splotches of pain. I stumbled to the ground, my head ringing. The metallic taste of blood filled my mouth. I raised my arms to protect my head from another blow. The intruder reached under his cloak, no doubt for a gun.

I tried to scream but couldn't find my breath. I had only wanted to help. Stupid girl. When had I been of any use to anyone?

The sound of racing footsteps came up the corridor behind me.

The intruder fled. I turned to see Richard running toward me, his face a mask of fury. The warmth of relief washed over me. I wanted to reach out for him, but I huddled aside, and he dashed passed, after the intruder.

The intruder darted into one of the rooms, and Richard followed. The sounds of crashing came from the chamber. I covered my mouth, willing Richard to be the victor, but I dared not interfere.

Richard strode back out a moment later, alone, his face still dark with anger. His dark hair was mussed, and a welt ran along his jaw. His gaze fell on me, and something in it shifted. He hurried forward.

"That man," I croaked out. "Is he…"

Richard stopped in front of me, his jaw twitching. Was he angry at me for being in the forbidden wing again? For breaking his vase?

I lowered my head. "I'm sorry, um, about the vase…"

He swept me to my feet and into an embrace. I was so stunned, I stood perfectly rigid for a moment. Then, I melted into his arms. My whole body trembled as images of the intruder—the murderer—flitted through my mind. Richard held me tighter, and my breathing slowed, my mind calmed. I rested my head against his chest, breathing deep the scent of horses and leather from his midnight ride. The rapid beating of his heart matched my own. He slowly released his grip on me and pulled back to inspect my face.

"Did he hurt you?" he asked, his voice rough.

"N-no. Though I'm certain he would have if you hadn't arrived. Where did he…"

"He made it to the window, and he had a horse waiting outside. I shouldn't have left you where you might be in danger."

"I thought I was meant to be bait," I said, trying to keep my voice light.

Richard paled at my words.

I put a hand on his arm and added more quietly. "I think I'm in danger no matter where I am."

I didn't want to point out that if I had stayed in my wing of the house, I likely would not have encountered the man. But Richard needed to know what the man had been doing.

"I heard a noise," I said, which was partly true. "And I saw him... Well, his cloaked form again, though I'm certain it was the same man. I think he was in the library."

Pain lanced over Richard's features, followed by fury. He crunched his foot on one of the broken pieces of vase and ground it into the rug. "Why can he not leave her in peace?"

"Perhaps she had something else he wanted? Something that would provide a clue to his identity?"

"It's been a year. If we were going to find such a clue, we would have done so. Why stir anything up? Does he think he...he owns her and all that is hers after..."

His voice cut off, and he only shook his head, the grief in his eyes so deep that I had to look away. I wanted to comfort him, but what could I say? I was more certain now that some clue to Eleanor's killer lay in her library, but Richard was correct: it made little sense to come looking for it after so long, drawing attention to it.

Unless my intruding on the library had somehow drawn his attention to it. I had spoken about it with the Reeves, and though I denied using the library, Mary no doubt crafted some strange rumor about it.

"I'm so sorry," I whispered.

He slowly pulled his expression back into one of stony calm. "Let me see you safely to your chambers. I'll send Walters to watch your corridor."

I glanced around for Eleanor's lights, but they had vanished as soon as Richard appeared. No, they vanished after they had swarmed the intruder. Had that cost Eleanor something? A flesh and blood guardian was no doubt better than a ghostly one.

"Thank you," I whispered.

Richard stared at me for a moment longer, then he offered his arm. I grabbed hold, grateful for his solid presence—better than Walters or Eleanor. But I could not have him for my protector. His whole focus was on solving Eleanor's mystery. I couldn't take him away from that, even if I wanted to. And unmasking the killer would keep me safe as well.

We walked in silence down the dark corridor. What was there to say?

When we reached my room, Richard motioned for me to stay quiet and opened the door. He pulled a pistol from under his coat and slipped inside. I had not thought of the possibility of the intruder finding me there. I shivered and wrapped my arms around myself, standing alone in the dark corridor.

Finally, Richard kindled a light in the chamber and beckoned me in.

"It's safe," he said.

I hurried in for the refuge of the light. Neale stood in the room, frowning.

"Wait!" he said, holding out a hand. He hurried to the dressing screen and looked behind it. His shoulders relaxed. "Nothing. But that's a strange place for a dressing screen."

"I—I moved it. I did not like the picture."

He looked at the painting, confused. "Hades and Persephone? Eleanor chose that one."

My face warmed. I didn't want to insult her. "I found the theme unsettling."

His features softened. "I see. I suppose it could be. Eleanor liked the story, though."

"She did?"

He nodded. "She pointed out it was Demeter, not Persephone who objected to the union. She thought Persephone ate the pomegranate seeds on purpose to bind herself Hades. After all, he made her a powerful queen. It was her mother who was controlling her."

"Oh! I had never thought of it that way."

I peeked past him to study the picture afresh. Yes, Hades carried Persephone in his arms, but she leaned against his chest, and her arm was slung around his neck. It was a dynamic scene—a passionate one—but Persephone did not look frightened. Perhaps the story had not been what I imagined. Perhaps Persephone had written her own future.

We both stared at the picture a moment longer, then Richard glanced at me. We stood in silence, and I wished I could read the thoughts behind his curious gaze. Finally, he bowed.

"Good night," he whispered.

He closed the door softly, but it caused the candles to

flicker. As they did, the shadows played over Persephone's face, and I wondered what happiness she had found with her shadowy husband.

CHAPTER 16

The next morning, I was surprised to find Richard at the table, apparently waiting for me. We had never breakfasted together. I took a moment to smooth my hair back in its loose chignon, then took my seat. He nodded and set aside his London newspaper.

"I have been thinking about your chamber," he said.

"Oh?" I asked.

"I don't want you so far from me. Um, your chamber, I mean." Red crept into his cheeks. "It will be easier to protect you if you're closer. If you don't object, I'll arrange for you to sleep in my wing of the house. The servants know about the intruder, so the change shouldn't arouse suspicions. I have already warned them to be more vigilant."

He didn't meet my eyes as he spoke, keeping his attention on his cold chicken and strawberry preserves. Did I want to be closer to him? I remembered how it felt to be held in his arms, and warmth poured through me, brighter than summer sunshine. I did want to be closer. But I had to be cautious. Practical. Our marriage would end, and I would not always have Richard Neale to rely on.

"Many nights you are not in the house," I said quietly. "So, it does not matter where I sleep."

He frowned at his plate. "It is easier to guard one wing than two. I have been short on servants since…since my sister's death. Even if I am not here—especially if I am not here—I would feel easier knowing that you are better protected."

That was a practical answer, and I couldn't find an argument against it.

"Then I think I should be closer." I sipped my tea. A buzz of excitement hummed through me. Only—I was sure—because moving closer to Richard would make it easier to investigate the library. "I didn't have an opportunity to ask: was your ride last evening productive?"

"Not as much as I would like. Tonight, we're trying something different."

"We?" I asked, imagining myself in a mask, holding a pistol.

"Yes. We're attending the Reeves' dinner party."

"Really?" I tried to hide my disappointment.

"You said you were lonely. I have been strict in mourning for my sister, but we will use our marriage as an excuse to begin attending limited social functions."

I leaned in. "What is your true objective, then?"

He tilted his head nearer. "The Reeves will have a large

party—many of them the same people who were there...that night. I wish to observe them."

I sensed that there was more to his plan than just observing, but I was happy that he was involving me at all, so I didn't press for more information.

After breakfast, I told Jane about our upcoming change in sleeping arrangements. She grinned widely at the news and bustled about to pack my things and make me presentable for a dinner party. I still had a lavender dress from mourning my father, which seemed appropriate to acknowledge the sister I would never meet. At least not in the flesh. We spent the day updating the style to be fitting for my role as Lady Neale—one I felt poorly prepared to play. But I did not want to disappoint Richard.

I HURRIED down the stairs to meet Richard for the dinner party. He waited near the front door, his expression indifferent once more. I hesitated, sorry that the more friendly Richard had vanished. He glanced up, then looked again. His eyes brightened, dispelling the indifference.

"Lady Neale," he said, sounding pleased.

I flushed with pleasure and curtseyed. "My lord."

He smiled. "I believe we are ready for the Reeves."

We sat across from each other in the carriage, both watching out the window, alone with our thoughts. My gaze drifted from time to time to Richard, his expression varying between a slight smile and a worried frown. I wondered again what he was planning.

The carriage delivered us to the Reeves' estate shortly before the dinner was to start. If Briarwood had disappointed my Gothic fancies, the Reeves' house exceeded them—a perfect crumbling country pile for a country squire. Parts of it may have dated to the Norman invasion, and new sections had been added haphazardly across the centuries: one portion Tudor, another Baroque. None were quite at harmony with each other, as if only custom held them together.

Richard offered his arm. I took it, feeling a jolt of heat at our nearness. My pulse picked up as he guided me inside. Here, my Gothic hopes were dashed. The interior was as bright as possible with the odd arrangement of windows, and the furnishings simple and modern.

We greeted Mrs. Reeves, and she gave us a tight smile. "Lord Neale. I was...pleased to receive your acceptance. We have not seen you in some time."

"I have been in mourning, naturally. But now, I need to introduce my wife to the neighborhood."

She smiled and curtseyed to me. "Of course. Lady Neale, it's a pleasure to see you again."

I returned the curtsey—but not too deeply. I was the local lady now.

She turned back to Richard. "Let me again extend my condolences on your sister."

Richard bowed his head. His grief was evident and sincere. I wondered why he was putting himself through what was obviously a painful experience—what did he really hope to learn here?

I was surprised and pleased to see Captain Reeves among the guests. He met my eyes and gave a slight smile of acknowledgement, but he waited until we were introduced to say anything to me, and then it was only politeness. It was for the best. It would be odd to be on friendly terms with another man, and the look my husband gave the captain was not kind.

Mrs. Reeves called for the ladies, and we followed her into the dining room without the men. Even from my limited experience with Society, I knew this to be an old-fashioned custom. She directed me to the seat next to her, and Mademoiselle Carriere beside me, with Mrs. Palmer and the other ladies farther down the table. I had no chance, then, to know Mrs. Palmer better and convince her to take me as a lady's companion when this farce with Richard ended.

When Mr. Reeves entered with the men, he sat with Richard at the other end of the table. I glanced down the room in frustration. Now I wouldn't know what Richard was doing, and I wouldn't be able to help. With a chill, I realized that someone at this table might be Eleanor's murderer. I smoothed out my napkin to still my nervous fingers.

The Comte de Carriere sat beside Richard. I would have thought a comte outranked a baron, but maybe it was because the comte was foreign. Mr. Palmer was next, with John Reeves and Captain Reeves across from me. I could watch the two young Reeves men, at least, so perhaps I could be useful to Richard after all.

I smiled at Mademoiselle Carriere. "I am glad to see you again, Mademoiselle."

She waved her napkin. "Oh, please, call me Ghislaine," she said, her French accent thick. "We are to be neighbors, and I love talking to new people. They are always interesting, do you not agree?"

"Always?" I asked, wondering if she could possibly be sincere.

"Of course! They have new stories to tell. I love stories. Don't you?"

"I have found lately that I do," I admitted.

John Reeves leaned toward Ghislaine. "I refuse to believe that you find all stories interesting." He flicked his gaze toward his sister Mary seated down near Mr. Reeves' end of the table.

The comte at that moment burst into an enthusiastic tale of his meeting with Marie Antoinette, embellishing it with descriptions of jeweled gowns, sumptuous delicacies built of sugar, and many compliments from the late queen to himself —all no doubt fabrications. Mary and Louisa leaned forward, eager for every word, but Richard wore his most indifferent mask, the elder Mr. Reeves appeared more interested in his wine than the story, and Mr. Palmer, on the comte's other side, looked like someone had fed him sour gooseberries.

"What an *extraordinary* honor to be so singled out," Mr. Palmer grumbled. "You have lived a charmed life—as you tell the tale."

The comte smirked and displayed his broad hand. "Do you see this ring?"

At that, the elder Mr. Reeves' head jerked up.

The comte flashed a ring set with a large, red stone. "The

dear Princesse de Lamballe gave me this jewel from her own hand before the wicked revolutionaries carted her to La Force Prison."

Mr. Reeves shook his head and returned his attention to his wine. Richard, however, studied the ring with almost as much interest as Mary and Louisa.

Mr. Palmer sneered. "The Princesse's fingers grew prodigiously in her last days, if that was hers. I met her when she visited Bath, and she had lovely, delicate hands then."

The comte's eyes flashed. "What tricks an old man's memory might play! It has been many seasons since the Palmers had the means to mingle with the *beau-monde*, has it not?"

Uncomfortable silence settled over the room. Mr. Palmer's face flushed to his graying hair. Mrs. Palmer went pale and set down her napkin.

The comte smiled at the ring. "But of course, I had her gift fitted to my hand. I carry on for the memory of those who are fallen."

John rolled his eyes and mumbled, "I wish he would take his carrying-ons somewhere else."

Ghislaine pouted at him. "You are sometimes too unkind. Too ready to be displeased. You will make a very poor husband."

"How unfortunate for you," John sneered.

My eyes widened.

"Oh, didn't you know?" John asked, twirling his port in his glass and glancing at his mother. "Our parents desire a match between us."

Ghislaine wrinkled her nose. "It is of all things the most unpleasant idea."

"At least we can agree on that." John toasted her and drained his cup.

Captain Reeves shook his head and gave me a look which said, *You see why I wander the woods.*

Mrs. Reeves sighed. "I apologize for my son's wicked tongue, Lady Neale. Sometimes young people do not appreciate the wisdom of their elders."

"Let us speak of something more pleasant," Ghislaine said. "More stories. The captain has many."

John groaned. "We have heard them all by now. Lady Neale must have something fresh to speak of."

My cheeks warmed. He had either forgotten or did not care that most of my recent history was scandalous.

"I have heard you met the highwayman," Ghislaine breathed out. "This is true, *non*?"

"It is," I said. Now I could throw suspicion away from Richard. I told a greatly exaggerated account of the encounter, emphasizing the man's *blue* eyes, thin frame, and airy voice.

"It is most romantic!" Ghislaine exclaimed when I recounted how he had kissed my hand.

I smiled, my mind drifting back to the way Richard had looked at me that first encounter. "I suppose it was."

I noticed Richard watching my performance, but when I caught his eye, he quickly looked away.

"Terrifying," Mrs. Reeves muttered.

Mrs. Palmer, on the other side of Ghislaine, gave me a

conspiratorial smile. What had she told me? We must take back our stories.

Feeling bold, I went on. "Lately, though, I have been interested in eerie stories. Ghosts. Surely, there must be some in this neighborhood?"

"*Oui!* Miss Neale knew of many. She could tell me such tales that made the hairs raise on my arms." She held out her delicate arm as if to demonstrate. "Do you believe in ghosts, Lady Neale?"

"I rather think I do. In fact, I would love to hear more about Miss Neale's ghost stories."

"If only I could remember them!" Ghislaine sighed. "Then I would not have to fear disappointing my new friend!"

Captain Reeves smiled sadly. "I'm afraid, Mademoiselle, that Miss Neale was teasing you. She loved to invent stories to make her friends happy."

Ghislaine narrowed her eyes. "But she did not spin them from the air like fairy gold. Even the best embroidery must start with cloth and thread. If you could read them you would see."

That line of thinking drew too much attention to Eleanor's library—and might draw the intruder back as well.

"Ghislaine," I said quickly. "I have always wanted to visit France, and that may not be possible anytime soon. Perhaps you can tell me more about it?"

The young lady was happy to oblige, and the rest of the dinner passed peacefully enough.

Just before the women withdrew to leave the men to their drinks, Richard slipped out of the room. Ah, now he was enacting his mysterious plan. He said he was looking for answers. Did that mean he would sneak around the house? It wasn't my place to tell him what to do, but that didn't mean I had to sit there and smile and wait for the embarrassment of being told that my husband had been caught prying in his host's house.

When the women exited the dining room, I excused myself to Mrs. Reeves and slipped off on my own, hurrying through the corridors in search of Richard. I peeked into the study and the library—places I thought he was most likely to find the kind of answers he was looking for—but they were empty. There were, however, several bedrooms in the next corridor, and one of them was cracked open with sounds of shuffling coming from within. I might risk seeing more than I wished to, but it seemed that everyone else was in the drawing room. Everyone except my husband.

I peeked into the room. It was clearly a lady's room, and Richard was making himself at home. I felt sick at the first suspicions that crossed my mind. But he was alone, rifling through... a jewelry box.

This was almost worse.

"Richard!" I hissed.

He whipped around and glared at me. "What are you doing in here?"

"What am I... What are *you* doing? Do you want to be arrested?"

He pressed his lips together and turned back to the jewelry. "If I'm caught, you can have the marriage annulled."

The old accusations rippled through my mind. *Thief. Thief. Thief.* Heat bubbled up from my stomach, and I curled my hands into fists, "And my name ruined forever. Thank you! And if you're not caught, they will blame some poor innocent maid—"

"If I find and take what I'm looking for, no one will dare report it."

I looked around the room. "This is Ghislaine's chamber. You think she could have killed your sister? I thought the killer was a man."

"She could be in league with the killer. I won't know until I've searched *everyone's* jewels."

I thought back to the unpleasant scene at supper. "The comte's ring?"

"Not Eleanor's. A fake, though." His voice sharpened. "I know one when I see one."

I nodded, then hurried over to open a chest of drawers.

"What are you doing now?" Richard whispered.

"Helping! The longer you take, the more likely you are to be caught. I do not want to be accused again of theft, not after my father..."

His eyes widened slightly. Had he forgotten? Perhaps, since he had enough of his own troubles to keep his mind busy.

A noise in the corridor made us both freeze. The sound of footsteps approached, and someone paused by the barely-open door.

Richard grabbed my hand as if to guide me... Where? We were trapped. About to be caught. And with my father's history, everyone would say that I had followed after him. Bad blood. Richard could say he had come to try to stop me...

He pulled me aside, as if shielding me with his body. I

wanted to bury my face in his chest, to avoid the accusations that were certain to come.

But then he wrapped an arm around my waist and drew me tight against him. I stared up into his dark eyes, and he leaned closer, his gaze traveling my face and ending on my lips. My mouth parted, but I couldn't look away. He lowered his face so his lips were nearly on mine, and we stood like that for what felt like a lifetime, my heartbeat thundering in my ears.

"I'm sorry," he whispered.

He buried his face in my neck, his breath warm on my skin. I didn't understand what he was doing, but I was confused and warm and a little light-headed, and I suddenly didn't care, just wanted to fall into the sensation of being held so tightly.

"Oh!" came a voice from behind me.

Richard looked up, loosening his grip on me, though I worried if he let go, my legs would give out and land me on the rug.

"Forgive me," he said over my shoulder. "The door was open, and my wife and I just stepped inside for some...conversation."

I glanced up to see Ghislaine watching us with a sparkle in her eyes. She giggled. "Of course, you are only newly married! It is natural. Only, our hostess was concerned and wanted me to see if Lady Neale had become lost. The gentlemen will be joining us in the drawing room."

Richard looked down at me. I blinked, trying to clear my head, trying to understand the regret in his expression. "Then I suppose we must go."

I let him guide me out of the room, my face down and burning in embarrassment. Ghislaine was not a gossip like Mary Reeves, but news of this improper conduct would no doubt spread. It would make it more difficult to convince anyone our marriage was false and should be annulled. I was more steeped in scandal than ever, and we were no closer to knowing who had killed Eleanor.

CHAPTER 17

When we returned to the drawing room, I expected all eyes to turn to us. To my surprise and relief, the others were occupied with their own interests. Mr. and Mrs. Reeves played cards with Mrs. Palmer who, I noted, was very conservative with the coins she laid on the table. The younger members of the Reeves family gathered around the piano-forte and argued over which song Louisa should play. The comte and Mr. Palmer stood to one side in an awkward conversation.

"You should consider selling some of your stocks," Mr. Palmer said stiffly. "Certainly, you have no need of them."

The comte sighed. "Nor do you, when you cannot afford them. What, you would pay me on credit like I am a shop-keeper? No, you bore me now with these silly ideas."

Mr. Palmer cast his eyes down, and his posture sagged.

"People would say it was in bad taste to have dancing

tonight." Mary's voice cut through everything else. "Especially given the circumstances."

She shot a significant look at Richard.

Richard wore his polite mask, but I knew him well enough now to see pain in his eyes. It was not long before he made our excuses, and we escaped the Reeves' overheated rooms.

Richard and I sat in silence on the return to Briarwood, the only sounds the jingle of harnesses and the grind of the wheels on the hard-packed road. I caught him glancing at me, but he quickly looked away when I tried to meet his gaze. My heartbeat refused to settle. Was he also thinking of the warmth between us when we had been so near? Of how close our lips had been? I could still smell his scent on my gown, and it made it impossible to ignore him.

He helped me out of the carriage, the warmth of his touch reaching through my glove. He did not release my hand. I looked up at him.

He gave me a weighty glance. "Come with me."

Obviously, he meant more than going into the house. My throat was tight, but I nodded.

He guided me inside and toward his wing of the house. I hesitated, looking at him uncertainly. Was he showing me to my new chambers? But why did he look so serious and sad?

He glanced down and smiled slightly. "Don't be afraid. I want to show you something."

I nodded for him to lead the way.

He guided me to a picture hanging in the corridor. "This is...this is Eleanor."

His voice caught on the name, but he had spoken it to me

for the first time. The first time, I suspected, that he had spoken it to anyone for a very long time.

I turned from studying him to studying his sister. There were similarities, especially in the dark hair. Her eyes were bright, almost laughing. They reminded me of Richard when he was playing the highwayman.

"She's lovely," I said. And I meant it. Not just her face, which was pretty enough, but in what I had come to know of her.

He nodded. "The jewelry she wears in the picture. That is what the killer took."

I looked more closely. Yes, she wore a pearl necklace, and also a choker with a little cameo. Then she had a bracelet of red stones. Garnets, perhaps. Richard had taken Frances's garnet necklace. And Eleanor wore two rings. One with a pearl, and one with a little flower. Of course, a rose.

"If you are helping, I thought you should see. Now you know what we're searching for," Richard said quietly, near my ear.

I looked up at him, shy of the sorrow and vulnerability in his eyes. But this was a rare chance to ask questions. "Garnets. Like you took from Frances."

"Yes."

"What did you do with Frances's necklace?"

He grimaced and glanced away, embarrassment in his eyes. It was beneath a baron to take jewels from a lady, even to hide his real intention for holding up coaches. "Walters sells them to various pawn stores in London where the victims may regain their treasures if they wish. And I donate the money to the Foundling Hospital. Anonymously, of course. I never take anything that has real value."

I nodded and rubbed my mother's ring beneath my glove. "You did return my mother's ring."

"I had to be certain it wasn't Eleanor's. When it I knew wasn't, I sensed that you needed it."

"Yes. I have little of my mother. She loved beautiful things, but my father... He had to sell most of them."

"That is not your shame. It is his. At least you are not robbing people." His mouth turned up in a humorless smile.

"But my father did. And he didn't do it seeking to bring justice to a killer. He did it because he was weak and selfish."

Richard stared at the picture of his sister. "I didn't know your father. Maybe he is what you say. But you don't know how grief will fracture a person. Some break in neat ways that are easy to patch and continue on. But sometimes those breaks are deep and not so easy to repair."

I thought that over. Thought of my father weeping over my mother's grave. Drinking himself to sleep. Ignoring Julian and me. I could not doubt that he was broken.

"Thank you," I said. "That is a compassionate way to view it."

Richard shifted. "Eleanor was compassionate. When someone behaved badly, she would always make up stories to explain their bad behavior. Perhaps they frowned at everyone because they just received news that their child-hood friend had been guillotined in France. Or perhaps they slighted her because they have gone nearsighted from reading the personal ads looking for a lost lover."

He smiled—a sincere, sad smile. No masks.

A few faint lights gathered above his head for a moment, but they faded before he noticed. As if Eleanor couldn't bear to be near his grief.

"She thought the best of others," I said.

"Yes." His voice hardened. "And that's why it galls so much that someone took advantage of that kindness. It was my job to protect her. To shelter that innocence. And I failed."

I stood beside him, no words of comfort to offer. I looked into Eleanor's laughing eyes. "You were her guardian for many years."

"Yes," he said hoarsely.

"Then I think you did protect her innocence. You allowed her happiness and imagination to flourish under your watchfulness. And you will bring her killer to justice."

He stepped closer, his gaze tracing my face. "Why have you concerned yourself with her?"

"We're both being hunted by the same person. But it's more than that. I feel... I feel close to her. Like she's still here in this place." I didn't know how he would react to learning how literal I believed that to be. "I know she cared about you, and you about her. And... I care about you too."

Richard's eyes widened slightly at that, and he shifted away, his mask falling back into place. I winced inwardly. I had said the wrong thing. What had Richard done before he embraced me in Ghislaine's room? He had apologized. I had seen the regret in his eyes after. Love and affection were for beauties like my mother, never for plain and practical women like me. I must never forget that.

"I appreciate your concern and cooperation," Richard

said coolly. "Hopefully, we will have justice served and you delivered to safety soon." He gestured to the door just down the corridor from the painting. "That chamber will be yours now. It hasn't been used for many years, but Harris prepared it for you and informed Jane." He hesitated. "My rooms are just down the corridor. In case there is danger."

With that, he bowed and bid me goodnight. I watched him go, some deep longing tugging within me to call him back, but I did not dare do it. He was not mine to call. It was foolishness to even think of it. A sigh echoed down the empty corridor, and I was not sure if it was mine or Eleanor's.

CHAPTER 18

Richard vanished again the next day, and it was as if our conversation had not happened. As if he hadn't almost kissed me, hadn't spoken to me like a friend, and hadn't turned cold again.

Though, I was in the family wing of the house now. My chamber wasn't much different, though instead of a painting of Persephone, there was one of Athena. It showed the goddess with her spear and helmet providing direction to Ulysses on his journey home. Had Richard chosen a room with this painting intentionally?

It was a good reminder. Athena was not a goddess to be loved, nor was she as fierce as Ares or Poseidon. She was a guide. Distant and wise. I had to be the same. If only I could be as useful to Richard as my namesake was to Ulysses. My stomach tightened into a knot. The best I could do at the moment was to clean Eleanor's garden before winter set in.

Jane helped me dress, all aflutter about my new chamber and the possibility of ghosts. I made all the correct responses and then sent her about her work so I could go to the gardens alone.

As I weeded, I felt someone pass behind me, almost brushing my shoulder. I gave a start and looked up, expecting to see Richard glaring down at me. But no one was there. I shivered and glanced about.

"Eleanor?" I half-whispered.

I stood and stared down at the terraces below, spotting a figure wandering the lakeside. Captain Reeves. I lowered myself again behind the bushes.

"Is he friend or foe?" I asked the autumn garden air.

Browning leaves rustled on the rosebushes, though no breeze stirred.

Richard suspected Captain Reeves, but he suspected everyone—even Ghislaine. I had only seen genuine mourning from Captain Reeves—sorrow but not guilt.

"I don't think he killed you."

Warmth ran over me like an encouraging breeze.

"I will try to prove it then," I told Eleanor.

I organized my gardening tools and went down to the lake. Captain Reeves saw me coming and stood, ready to greet me when I arrived.

"Lady Neale." He bowed.

"Captain Reeves. I was sorry not to speak to you more at your uncle's dinner party."

"Yes. I'm afraid I find parties difficult now. In the past, Eleanor would have been there. I know she would want me to heal and find further happiness, but..."

Richard had said everyone fractured differently. Eleanor's death had left a deep gash in the captain's peace.

"But it is unsettled," I prompted. "Especially when one does not know what happened to her."

He nodded.

"And there are always regrets," I went on, thinking of my father. How I wondered sometimes if he would have been better if *I* had been better somehow. If I could have stopped his slide into notoriety.

"Only that I did not have more time with her." The captain stared up at the house. At the gardens. "That I did not save her."

"Do you have any mementos of her?" It was an abrupt, almost rude question, but I knew what I was looking for now.

He looked a little taken aback, but then he smiled. "She did gift me a lock of hair." He pulled a chain from under his shirt and showed me the simple locket with a dark curl caught in it.

"That is lovely. It must be difficult not to have anything else of hers," I prompted, though I did not expect him to suddenly admit that he had the rest of her jewelry. I was more interested in seeing if any flash of guilt crossed his face.

Captain Reeves studied the lock of hair. "I would love a miniature of her, but I never had one made, and I doubt her brother would give me one now."

"Perhaps he will someday soften to the idea." If we found the killer and proved it was not Captain Reeves. "Did she have any favorite trinkets or other things that would remind you of her?"

He considered for a moment. "I remember the little ring she wore often. And her mother's bracelet was dear to her. But those belong to her family, not to me."

"Of course."

Either he was a good liar, or he did not know those things were missing. Richard had kept it a secret. That was wise—the killer might be caught out that way.

"I'm sorry if it is painful to remember, but I would like to find answers. Eleanor should have justice, and I know it would set Lord Neale at peace."

He nodded. "She was not a vengeful person, but she wanted things to be good and fair. She believed in the good and fair. Sometimes..." He looked down. "Sometimes I imagine I sense her nearby, as though she lingers. If anything, I suspect she wishes for her brother to be at peace."

"I think she would want you to be at peace as well," I said. "And I do not think the idea that something of her lingers is foolish. Many days, I do not think I'm alone at Briarwood."

He gave me a quizzical look.

"When my husband must be away, I mean." I cleared my throat. "Can you tell me about that night? If it's not too painful..."

"I will try. It's been a year, but the memory is still clear. Too clear." He looked into the pond as if it were a mirror to the past. "Everyone local of consequence was there, and many friends and acquaintances from Bath made the journey as well. Eleanor's parties always...sparkled."

I nodded. My mother had been that way also.

"I danced with her. Twice. We were working up the courage to tell Lord Neale that our infatuation had grown serious. I was set to prove to him that I could provide for his sister, and that we would be happy together. She and I stepped into the corridor to discuss our plan. Her brother saw us and pulled her aside to lecture her about the impropriety of showing such favor to me. It was not as private as it ought to have been. They left each other angry, and she went out to the gardens."

I mulled that over. If Richard's last words to her had been angry ones, how much sharper his pain must be.

"She would not have been alone out there," I said. "Others must have gone to enjoy the air or the quiet."

His brow drew together. "Well, if she had been perfectly alone, she would have been safe. I knew she needed a moment, and I did not want to cause a greater scandal, so I did not follow. If only I had..."

He squeezed his eyes shut.

I put a hand on his arm. "You cannot blame yourself for the actions of a villain."

"Thank you," he whispered. "She was out there for a short time. Perhaps five minutes. There was a scream." He swallowed. "I was one of the first out, but Lord Neale was there before me. He was holding her and trembling. Eleanor was..." His voice caught. "The inquest said she had been strangled."

"There is no possibility it was an accident, then," I said softly. And I could see why it looked bad for Richard.

Captain Reeves only looked down and took deep breaths.

"Despite what others said, I saw the look of grief and distress on Lord Neale's face. He did not hurt her."

"Thank you for telling me," I said.

"I hope it helps her in some way, though it's hard for me to see what difference it will make. It has been a year, and the more time that passes, the deeper the crime is buried."

"Perhaps," I said. "But perhaps the memory of that night is smoldering in the guilty heart and will cause him to say or do something to expose his crime."

Captain Reeves nodded, but he looked bleak.

I chewed my lip. "Something that might be helpful, though no doubt difficult for you, would be to have an accounting of who was at the party and who you remember staying inside for certain."

"And therefore, who might have been outside at that time?" He looked thoughtful—something sparking in his sad eyes.

"Precisely. A magistrate may have done it at some point, as part of the inquest, but we don't know what he found."

Captain Reeves smiled a little. "My uncle was the magistrate who investigated. A touchy business, you can imagine. But I might be able to find the information he collected."

"Oh, that could be very helpful!"

"I'll see what I can do. For Eleanor's sake."

CHAPTER 19

I was surprised a few days later to receive a morning call from Miss Louisa and Mademoiselle Ghislaine.

"I hope you don't mind us calling again," Louisa said once I had them settled in the drawing room with tea. "I took you at your word that we would be welcome."

"Of course!" Richard would not like anyone prying into our lives, but I hoped to learn more from these gossipy ladies who had known Eleanor—and probably knew her killer without realizing it.

Louisa pulled something from her reticule—an envelope. "My cousin, Captain Reeves, asked me to deliver this to you. He said it was about Miss Neale. I wasn't certain... It was a delicate situation..."

"Oh, that was kind of you to bring it," I said quickly, happy to snatch the envelope from her. "I want to understand better the sister I will never have a chance to meet."

"Is it one of her stories?" Louisa asked, looking at the envelope almost hungrily. "I have missed her stories."

"If it is, I will share it with you," I said, knowing it was not.

"We could tell you more about her, too," Louisa said.

"You knew her as well?" I asked Ghislaine.

"*Oui.* We had visited our friends the Reeves last year as well, before the tragedy. Poor Eleanor! An English rose."

I nodded. "I would love to hear your stories about her, both of you."

"Stories!" Ghislaine laughed. "She was always telling stories. Sometimes we would make them up together."

Louisa clasped her hands in her lap. "I am too stupid to be much help, but Ghislaine and Eleanor created such adventures!"

"Oh, say no such things!" Ghislaine said. "You are not stupid. You were smart enough to enjoy our stories, to see the genius of them. All stories need an audience, do they not?"

Louisa flushed. "You are almost as kind as Eleanor. I do hope you become my sister."

Ghislaine sighed dramatically. "I would like you for a sister, but I am not so certain about your brother as a husband."

"If you both object to the match, I am surprised your parents are pressing it," I said carefully.

Ghislaine shrugged one shoulder. "My papa wishes for it. For me to be safely settled in England. Mr. Reeves is not so bad looking, but he would always be giving me the headache. Yet Papa is not used to anyone telling him *non*. And practical marriages are common, are they not?"

"They are."

Julian and Frances, for instance. Julian had sincerely liked Frances when they began courting. I had thought her a bit conceited but otherwise amiable. It was when Father died and everyone said that Frances would make or break our future that she became self-righteous and domineering. And Julian, drowning in debt and despair, drifted into the inevitable.

I wondered what made the Reeves wish for the match with Ghislaine, though. French nobility did not have the same importance now as a connection to English nobility would.

"Well," Ghislaine said. "If I wish to laugh at my silly husband, I can go back to the stories Eleanor and I wrote about John Reeves."

My eyebrows rose. "Mr. Reeves was in some of your stories?"

Louisa giggled. "Those were the best stories, when they used real people. Sometimes I could hardly tell what was true and what was false in them."

Ghislaine nodded. "That was all Eleanor. She was always thinking of stories about people."

I sat back, thinking. "Lord Neale mentioned that she always imagined the best of people."

Ghislaine smiled. "Oh, usually she did. But some of our stories were very Gothic."

"My favorite was when she imagined what happened to the missing maid," Louisa whispered.

"Missing maid?" I asked, then remembered that Jane had said something about that, and Harris had hinted at it as well. I had assumed that had happened after Eleanor's death.

"*Oui.*" Ghislaine leaned forward to whisper, "One of the girls just vanished—poof! It was the talk of the village until…"

Until Eleanor's death provided bigger gossip.

"She was distressed about it," Louisa said. "She was the lady of the house, after all, and she knew her brother hadn't…" She cleared her throat. "Well, she said the stories helped her think it through."

I nodded. "That makes sense."

"I felt like they helped me think, too," Louisa said softly. "Like when I listened to her stories, I wasn't so stupid, but things made more sense to me."

Ghislaine patted her hand. "It is strange, though. I have heard rumors that more maids have left from Briarwood since. People blame… Well, they say this place is cursed. The house does seem sad now, does it not?"

"I didn't know it before," I said, "But there is sorrow here. Grief lingers in places, I suppose. Perhaps, though, it would help to remember happier times. Please, tell me more of Eleanor."

I listened to their reminiscences, which painted more broad brushstrokes of Eleanor's happy nature but told me little of who might have hurt her. Behind my smile, my mind whirled. A maid had gone missing. Eleanor investigated, and then someone killed her. What did she find—what was the connection? If only she could speak and tell me what she had found.

But maybe she could! Her stories. Even if she had not left proper notes, her ideas would all be there in the stories she told, especially now that I knew what to look for. I was going to have to risk my husband's wrath again to find the clues she left me.

As much as I enjoyed Ghislaine and Louisa's friendliness, I was excited to see them out at the end of the visit. I needed to go back to the library. I had the letter from Captain Reeves and Eleanor's stories to keep me occupied.

But when I returned to the entrance hall, Richard stood guarding my way. Guilt flushed my cheeks. Did he know what I planned to do?

"Another visit from the Reeves?" he asked. He looked almost guilty himself.

"Yes. I know we must be cautious, but I don't think those two girls mean any harm. They are...cheerful."

"In a way little in this house is anymore," he said quietly.

"It is a house in mourning."

He nodded. "I...I didn't intend to eavesdrop, but I over-heard snatches of what they were saying. About Eleanor."

"Oh. I didn't mean to cause you more pain." I hoped he hadn't heard the hints about the missing maids and the curse on Briarwood.

"No." He sighed. "I think it was good. Healthy. Like letting a fresh breeze into a room that needs to be aired. I almost felt like she was here again, brought back to life by remembering."

I wet my lips, wishing I could tell him how true I believed that to be but afraid to offend or hurt him.

He stepped closer, his eyes finding mine. My breath caught, and I could not look away from his searching gaze. He placed a gentle hand on my elbow. "I am grateful to you. For breathing a bit of life back into this house. I suppose if Briarwood is cursed, it is because of the darkness I have brought to it."

"I don't think this place is cursed," I said. "It is only dimmed by a veil of grief."

"A shroud, you mean." His voice was quiet and bitter.

I tentatively placed my hand on his chest. "A heart that is broken and hurting is not dead. It can heal. It may bear scars, but it can also feel...feel happiness again."

Perhaps even love. But that love could never be for me. I looked into Richard's intense gaze, and my cheeks warmed, spreading a glow to my own aching heart.

Could it?

"Thank you," Richard said, his voice hoarse. "Thank you for returning some light to Briarwood."

He took the hand that rested on his chest and raised it to his lips, gently kissing my knuckles. Then he smiled sadly and strode away.

I placed my hand to my chest, trying to still my racing pulse. From the corner of my eye, I caught a sparkle of lights.

CHAPTER 20

I didn't feel right sneaking into Eleanor's library after that exchange, so I returned to my room and sat, lost in memories of Richard's dark eyes.

No, that was silly. Impractical. I shook myself and opened Captain Reeves' letter. As promised, he had delivered a list of names of those who attended the fateful party. It was several pages long, and I knew very few of them. I groaned. How was I going to learn about each of these people? If Richard had a copy of *The New Peerage*, I could investigate any of the families with noble connections, but what a chore it would be.

If only I could ask Richard for help, but I still didn't know how he would react to the extent of my personal investigations. He was taking his mask off in front of me more often, but he was just as quick to put it on again.

I stroked the back of my hand where he had kissed it, then shook my head at the memory. I was a foolish girl, not being practical at all. We were only working together to find a killer, and then all of this would be over. At least at this point, I trusted that Richard would help me find a position where I could be comfortable. He had a heart beneath his indifferent facade.

I sighed and went to work on the list, making notes on the guests I did know: the Reeves, the Palmers, some names I'd heard my father or brother mention. Time slipped past, until a tap sounded on the door.

I jumped and shoved the papers out of sight.

"Yes?" I called, still a little short on breath. What if it was Richard?

But Jane poked her head in. "Supper is ready, my lady."

I almost asked to take supper in my room so I could continue working, but Jane wore a broad grin. The look of anticipation in her eyes convinced me to come to the table. Maybe we were having something besides trout.

When we reached the dining room, Jane turned with a smile and walked away. I wrinkled my forehead. We had fallen into the habit of eating together. I peeked into the dining room.

Richard sat at the head of the table, dressed in his highwayman garb without the mask. He stood when I entered.

"I hope you don't mind," he said. "You did mention that you wanted company at meals, and I had time before I needed to ride out."

"Of course, I'm happy to see you!" In fact, my heartbeat had picked up, and I felt uncertain what to do with my hands, so I settled on trying to smooth down my chignon.

He motioned to the seat beside him, and I took it, folding my hands in my lap.

"I gathered from Cook that you might be tired of trout, so we're having pheasant. I hope that's acceptable."

"Oh, yes! I know trout is a practical meal because of the pond—"

"But you don't always have to be practical," Richard said softly.

"Don't I?" It came out as almost a plea.

"Not at Briarwood. You have already done so much, reminding me of things Eleanor would not want me to forget. Things I don't want to forget." He shrugged one shoulder. "In any case, I am hardly practical, so I don't see why you should be."

He carved the pheasant and handed me the plate. Our fingers brushed when I took it, and warmth rushed up my arm.

My cheeks burned. "I have been the practical one for so long, I don't what else I might be."

"Simply be Athena," he said.

I wrinkled my nose. Athena *was* practical. Nothing else. "I never cared for my name."

"Oh?" Richard studied me. "You seem wise to me."

I prodded the meat on my plate. "I'm not so certain. But it's more than that."

Richard's expression turned more serious. "What then?"

I hesitated. I had never spoken of this. It seemed so silly. So impractical. But there was something about the way he was watching, listening, as though nothing I could say would be too ridiculous.

I sighed. "Athena was the goddess of wisdom. She even took a helmet and spear and fought like a man. And she gained great respect that way, didn't she?"

Richard nodded.

"But...she was living in the world of the gods—the male gods. She was born from the head of Zeus. From the mind of a man. And she played the game of the male gods, gaining their respect by being what they expected. I feel like that is the game I have been playing, too. Trying to play a part written by someone else, in someone else's story." Guiding Ulysses on his adventure, not having one of her own.

I felt Richard's gaze on me, but I was too embarrassed to meet his eyes.

He cleared his throat. "I could argue that it shows how clever women are, that they can succeed at a game not designed to favor them," he said softly. "But I'd rather hear what name you would prefer."

"I don't mean I wish to be called by a different name, but some part of me—the part that was always required to sit quietly and be good and useful and practical..." My face heated, but I made myself go on. "That part of me wished I could tear my hair free from its braid or chignon and run outside. To be...be wild. To make my own kind of freedom instead of playing the game of others."

"You wish to be not Athena, but Artemis. The goddess of nature and the hunt."

"Yes," I said with more passion than I intended.

"As long as you are at Briarwood, I want you to feel free." He smiled a little. "You may even unbind your hair if you wish."

I dared to look up at him and saw that he was smiling—kindly, no mockery in his expression.

"Thank you," I whispered.

He toyed with his fork. "There is only one thing that troubles me."

"Yes?" I asked.

"Athena and Artemis... They are both maiden goddesses. Whether inside or outside of the other gods' games, they remained...independent."

"That is true." People might have respected Athena and Artemis, but they were not loved. "I suppose I have always known that I was going to have to forge my own path to happiness. There was little enough of it in my home, especially after my mother died."

"I see," Richard said softly. He was quiet for a long moment, not meeting my eyes. "But I do think that we can work well together? Even...even just for a time?"

"Oh, yes! I enjoy our time together."

"I am glad." But there was sadness in his voice.

He took my hand, rubbed his thumb over the back of it. Warm prickles raced up my arm. His face had gone very serious, but then he smiled—his highwayman smile.

"Then, I must leave you to ride my own course, but I will look forward to having someone to relate my adventures to when I return."

"I will enjoy hearing them."

He kissed my hand, lingering for a moment, then gave me a dramatic bow and swept away.

I listened to the sound of the door, straining to hear the beat of his horse's hooves as he left for his night of hunting.

If I was allowed to be Artemis, even just for a time, I had my own hunting to do.

I hurried to Eleanor's library and dared to light a candle. I did not think Harris or anyone else would challenge me now. I sat at Eleanor's desk.

"Help me to find whatever clues you left," I whispered to the room. To Eleanor. "I will find the voice that the killer stole from you.

The candle wavered and then leapt up more brightly.

I nodded firmly and began to sort through the papers, making two stacks. One was of the more light-hearted stories about girls who charmed dragons or outwitted fairies. A few clearly mocked the Reeves, especially Miss Mary and Mr. John Reeves, portraying them as vain or foolish and teaching them a well-deserved lesson at the end. Louisa and Ghislaine might have helped with those. Would the tales have upset any of the antagonists badly enough to kill Eleanor over them? I considered the stories. Probably not. They weren't flattering, but they weren't libelous, either.

In the other stack, I placed stories with a more serious tone. The Red Riding Hood story. Another that reminded me of the Biblical story of the prodigal son who went into the world and wasted his inheritance before coming home to beg forgiveness. In this story, however, the prodigal returned not to seek forgiveness, but to steal his brother's inheritance as well. I frowned over that one. Was Captain Reeves meant to be the returning prodigal? If so, it was a strange thing for her to write about someone she was supposed to love.

One of her fairy tales was about an evil sorcerer who lived in a castle in the woods. He would set out sweet things to lure girls to the castle. Once he had them there, he transformed into a wolf. Some of the girls were able to flee from the wolf, but others he captured and devoured.

I considered that story for a long time. That could be about the missing maid. Unfortunately, it did not provide many clues. Another hint that a wolf lurked among the sheep, and that it was using sweet promises to lure its victims in. Who would that be? John Reeves perhaps? Or maybe Captain Reeves, if Eleanor had discovered that he was deceitful. But that didn't feel right.

"Who was your wolf, Eleanor?"

The door slammed open, and the candle flickered, almost blown out by the gust. I quickly sheltered it with my hand and swung to face...

Richard, still dressed as a highwayman. I had overstayed my welcome.

"Athena. I know I granted you freedom, but—" He gaze settled on the desk, his eyes full of pain.

"I have taken advantage of that offer, far beyond what you intended. I know it. But please, listen to what I have found about Eleanor."

He went very still at that, his face once again a mask.

My heart ached at seeing his coldness, but I drew a long breath. "I realized there might be another way to discover the killer. He was no stranger, I think we both agree."

He nodded once.

"And...perhaps you knew that your sister liked to write stories about her acquaintances. Miss Louisa mentioned it to me."

Richard nodded again, looking less cold, more thoughtful this time.

"I know most of the stories were in good humor, even positive. But sometimes, something more leaked through. Something that troubled her. Maybe something she knew about that troubled someone else as well."

I held out the story about the wolf.

He stared at the papers for a long time, as if frightened of what he might see. Then, he slowly reached out and took them. He slowly paged through the story, pain in his eyes as he read over the words.

"Only a fairy story," he said, though his voice was tight.

"I don't think it is. She was very creative, but her creativity was in looking at the obvious in new ways, not spinning tales out of moonlight and air. I think this story is about... about the maids that have gone missing from Briarwood."

"And I am the wolf, I suppose," he snapped.

"Did you offer lures to innocent girls?" I kept my voice steady, but it was difficult. I didn't believe he was the wolf, and I didn't want to be proven wrong.

"Never," Richard said coldly.

"I didn't think so. Your sister always portrays you heroically. You are the knight, not the wolf, regardless of rumors. But your sister found the wolf. And the wolf killed her."

Richard's fingers tightened on the papers, crumpling the edges. He stared at the words for a long time. Then he shoved the story back at me.

"Why did she not tell me if she had discovered some danger?" His voice was pained.

"I don't know," I whispered. "Maybe she didn't realize how serious the danger was. Maybe she was going to tell you, and—"

"And the killer silenced her so she would never have the chance." He balled his fist. "I will find the wolf and skin him!"

"Can you tell from the story who it might be? You know the people of this area better than I do."

He held out his hand, and I passed the papers back to him. After skimming through it again, he shook his head. "A sorcerer? Sweet promises? It is not very specific. I wonder… I wonder if she was not yet certain. She had suspicions, but did not want to accuse anyone wrongly. She would hate to tell false tales about anyone."

I nodded. "That sounds reasonable. Does this help your quest?"

"It confirms that the person we're searching for is someone close. Someone she knew. Maybe someone she trusted and did not want to suspect."

His eyes narrowed. I guessed he was thinking of Captain Reeves again. I didn't think him guilty, but we had to be wary, because Eleanor's hesitation might have cost her her life.

"There might be something in more of the stories," I suggested. "I have not yet read them all."

Richard glanced at the desk and wet his lips. "I…will leave that task to you. It is very painful to read her words again when her voice is no longer here."

I nodded, sorry for his pain and yet glad I could finally help in some way.

He gave me a curious look. "How did you know where to find her stories?"

I drew a deep breath. I needed to tell him. "I think she guided me to them."

His forehead wrinkled. "My sister?"

"I don't think she's as far from you as you might think. I think she wants the truth to come out, and she wants you to have peace."

His expression softened for a moment, but then he shook his head. "I don't believe in fairy stories, or in ghost stories. But I do believe in finding justice." He met my eyes for a moment, dark pain reflected in them. "Good night, Athena. And... thank you."

Warmth poured through me at his gratitude. I was no longer useless! I smiled and returned to my task with renewed energy, burning my candle long into the night.

CHAPTER 21

Richard met me for supper again the next evening. I took my seat beside him, my heart fluttering. The meal on the table consisted of roast pork and apples. My mouth watered at the scent. What a relief to have another respite from trout!

Richard once again carved a piece and set it before me.

"Thank you, my lord."

He shook his head. "We need no such formality. Richard will do."

"Very well, my... Richard."

My Richard? My cheeks warmed at the verbal stumble. Richard was not mine. We were becoming friends, and I was glad he found me helpful now, but I was not a great beauty destined to call anyone *mine*.

I cleared my throat and asked softly, "Was your ride productive?"

He glanced about to be certain the servants had left us alone, then shook his head. "It begins to feel futile. Did you... learn anything?"

"Not yet. It might go more quickly if you helped. I understand the task is vexing for you, but I know little of the members of Society."

His eyes had been distant, pained, but then he focused on me with curiosity. "Were you not often in London?"

"No." I speared a soft apple. "Mother died before I would have been out, and Father...didn't find the time for such things."

"Hmm. I'm sorry your interests were ignored, but most of Society is hardly worth knowing."

"I doubt I would have taken to it anyway. My mother was beautiful, and always dancing, surrounded by admirers, but that was never me."

He set down his fork. "By your own admission, you didn't have the opportunity to find out."

I remembered again sneaking into the ballroom and my mother's look of dismay. My throat tightened. "It doesn't matter now," I whispered.

Richard continued to study me. "You regret the lost opportunity?"

"I don't know." I set my own fork down, irritated. Why? None of it mattered. The chance was past, and I would never get it back. "I've seen how cruel Society can be. Most of it, I do not regret. But..." I tapped my fingertips on the white linen tablecloth.

"But?" Richard asked softly.

I sighed. "I enjoyed dancing, and my mother was a fine dancer. I might have liked to dance at Almack's."

"You don't need Almack's to dance."

I sighed. "It's not about Almack's specifically. It's about being respectable. Accepted. You know about my father. *Everyone* knows about him. But my mother was a lady. She doesn't deserve to have her memory tarnished by association with my father's actions. I want to...to redeem her."

"That's noble of you." Richard looked thoughtful. "Did your mother care so much about her reputation?"

"I don't know. It was always sterling, so there was nothing about it to pain her." Again, her look of dismay when I entered the ballroom flashed in my mind. "No, that's not entirely true. I think she did care, and all this gossip would pain her."

Richard nodded. "It's natural to care when people say vile things about those you love. It has been difficult since Eleanor died. I try not to listen, but I can't ignore it all. I can't help but wonder if some of the things they say are true."

"The worst of it is not!" I said, then bit my lip. Did he know the worst of it? I was certain there were rumors about me I did not want to hear.

"The worst of it? That I strangled her with my own hands?" His voice was tight, and he pushed his plate away. "I know what they say. I also know they accuse me of controlling her too much. And that...what if that was true? What if, in some way, I *was* strangling her?"

He frowned, brooding, and my heart ached for him. I grabbed his hand, and his eyebrows rose in surprise.

I tightened my hold on his hand. "She didn't feel that

way. I have been reading her stories. You were her hero, her protector. Never a villain."

"I hope…I hope that was always true." He swallowed and looked down at our hands, the hard lines of his expression softening. "The gossip is bad enough for me, and I have my title and my sex to protect me. I know women are in a more fragile position. If anything comes of this misadventure, I'm glad that my title might do you some good as well. Offer some protection."

I released his hand and glanced down, flustered. "I simply try not to care. It is…more practical that way."

He smiled a little. "I suppose it is sometimes helpful to be practical, then." He touched my fingers, sending little flower-petal flutters swirling in my chest. "I have a very impractical idea, though."

"Oh?" I asked, trying to find my breath. "I do recall someone giving me permission to be impractical."

"Come!" He took my hand and led me toward the ballroom.

I followed, aware of nothing except the strong but gentle clasp of Richard's hand around mine.

He released me when we reached the ballroom, but he watched me expectantly. Flustered and uncertain, I took a moment to admire the painted ceiling and mirrored walls once again. The watching eyes no longer seemed so disap-proving. "It's a lovely room."

"Have you learned to waltz?" Richard asked.

I gave a start. "I've heard it is an indecent foreign dance. I suppose you know it?"

"Of course. I learned it overseas, when such travel was

possible. And now I will teach it to you. No—before you object, there is no one around to observe, and we are a married couple, after all."

I flushed up to the roots of my hair. But he was right: Who would know? And I *did* want to dance in that lovely room. It was my turn to be impractical. "Very well. Teach me."

He grinned his mischievous highwayman's smile. "Excellent. I place my hand on your waist like this."

He wrapped his arm around me and held me close. Indecent indeed. Scandalous. My heartbeat thrummed.

"Then you place your hand on me, thusly."

He guided my hand to his shoulder. We stood in a distant embrace, warmth flowing between us.

"And then we join our free hands," he said, offering his.

I took it, his grip strong but not crushing. Reassuring.

"And we turn to the beat."

"There is no beat," I whispered.

"No?" he asked, watching me closely, questioning. He took my hand from his waist and placed it on his chest, over his heart. "There is that one."

I looked up at him, my mouth gone dry. Keeping a firm grip on me, he guided me through the turning steps: one-two-three, one-two-three, one-two-three. I let my hand slide back down to his waist. I wasn't sure where to look, but somehow, I ended up meeting his gaze as we twirled through the ballroom. His eyes lit with a smile as they had when he held up our carriage outside Bath. We found a rhythm between the two of us. Was it my imagination, or did lights twinkle around us? It felt like soaring through a starry sky.

"Now, this isn't too scandalous, is it?" he asked, his deep voice resonating through me.

"I think it's very scandalous," I said, a little breathlessly.

"Really? Well, you couldn't enjoy this kind of dancing at Almack's."

"I imagine not." Maybe Almack's was not such a wonderful place.

He twirled me around. "I'd wager you're just as fine a dancer as your mother."

"You are teasing me." I sighed. "She was beautiful."

"I cannot imagine she was any more beautiful than you."

I blinked and looked for some mockery in his expression, but there was none. "But..."

But Miss Davidson always insisted I was not beautiful. That was why my mother did not want me. Why no one could love me.

I shook my head. "You have been away from Society for too long."

"I don't think so," he said, his voice low. "In fact, I recall something else you can't do at Almack's."

"What's that?" I asked.

He pulled me closer, bringing the dance to an end. I stared up at him, excited and a little frightened by the intense look in his eyes. He stroked back a stray curl that had fallen into my face. A pleasant shiver ran through me, and I closed my eyes. Then he pulled the pins from my chignon, letting my hair fall free.

"Artemis needn't keep her hair pinned back," Richard whispered, his words husky.

I opened my eyes to meet his, and my gaze traveled to his lips. He leaned nearer. My breath caught, and I wanted to pull him closer, but I couldn't move. This was impossible. I was not beautiful. Richard could not love me. I could not let myself love him. He would leave me alone, just as my mother had. Just as everyone did.

He sighed and pulled away. "Artemis deserves to be free."

"Free?" My voice cracked.

"What did you plan for…for after this?"

I assumed he did not mean after supper. I cleared my throat. "I had considered becoming a lady's companion."

"Would that make you happy?"

I should have said yes, but it stuck in my throat.

"If we catch the killer," Richard said, his words coming fast. "You would be safe. You could stay here. I would not ask anything of you—nothing more than friendly companionship—but I could continue to offer you the protection of our false marriage."

Friendly companionship. False marriage. The words punched my breath away. I had thought for a moment he found me attractive—that he wanted to kiss me—but it was only my sheltered naivety misunderstanding his kindness. Foolish girl.

"My lord?" Walters called from somewhere in the house.

Richard huffed and stepped away. A chill rushed over me. My hand slipped from his, and I clenched it into a fist, wishing I could grasp his waistcoat and keep him close.

"I'm here!" Richard called. He looked back to me. "Perhaps we should continue this... conversation later?"

I nodded, but I wasn't sure what I would say. He offered to let me stay at Briarwood—but still not truly as his wife. I was in danger of giving too much of my heart to him. Would it be more exquisite torture to be far from him, or to be near him every day and know he did not love me?

CHAPTER 22

Jane was unusually quiet as she arranged my hair the next day. I thought at first she had picked up on my pensive mood. My interrupted conversation with Richard still hung over me, and my heart was bruised and aching.

Then, Jane cleared her throat. "My lady?"

"Yes?" I tried to meet her eyes in the mirror, but she avoided my gaze.

"I'm afraid you will be displeased, but I must tell you."

My stomach tightened. "Please do, Jane."

"I've been hearing rumors around here. Of course, maids always do." She wet her lips.

I braced myself and nodded for her to go on.

"I was curious about those maids who left so suddenly."

"The lambs," I whispered.

"What?"

"Like lost lambs," I said, holding back any explanation until I heard what she had to say.

"Maybe more than you realize. Maids are so vulnerable. And I haven't seen any ghosts or anything else frightening here. I wondered what would make them run."

"Yes, go on."

"It seems they had been happy here, and then suddenly they grew uneasy. Jumpy. One girl was sometimes seen in tears, and then she suddenly vanished. That was what they had in common—they all left suddenly."

"Did they leave belongings behind?" A poor maid would not make it far without her things.

"No. They took everything and vanished in the night."

"Hmm." Maybe they ran for safety, then. And that might mean they were out there still, alive with their secrets. "You have suspicions about what frightened them away?"

Jane was silent for a long moment. She finished pinning my hair into place. "Often, that sort of thing happens because a powerful man is making inappropriate gestures."

I felt sick at the idea. Richard told me he had offered no lures to innocent girls, but would he think of maids that way? And was it any of my business?

"I considered your husband first," Jane said quietly, "but I think I can absolve him. I have not seen nor heard even a whisper of anything inappropriate from him since I arrived."

I felt hopeful at that. "Though not much staff is left at Briarwood."

She gave me the closest to a condescending look I'd ever seen from Jane. "The staff knows things, my lady. A master who regularly abused the maids might pass himself off as a gentleman to his peers, but the staff would know."

I sighed in relief. "Not Richard then." I cocked my head. "But then who?"

"I don't know, my lady."

"But you want to know."

She hesitated, then nodded, her eyes fierce. "I do. But I do not want to displease or shame you with unseemly investigations."

"You would not shame me," I said. "In fact, I think it would honor this household and the name of Lord Neale if we discovered who has been trifling with his staff. Yes, Jane, help me find the wolf hunting the lambs."

"Yes, my lady!" her eyes flashed with determination. Then she smiled ruefully. "Speaking of wolves... the Reeves sent a card that they are coming to visit today."

A chill ran up my spine. "You think John Reeves is a wolf?"

She met my gaze in the mirror this time. "I know the Reeves' staff is unhappy. Some of the Reeves are...difficult, at least. John Reeves might be a cad. Or Captain Reeves."

I winced a little at that, but I could not let imagined fondness between Eleanor and the captain exonerate him. "See what you can discover. But be discreet, Jane. This could be dangerous, and I don't want you harmed."

"I lived with Frances. I can be discreet. Now, you must go face the lady wolves."

I nodded, though really it was only the eldest that concerned me.

I awaited my guests in the drawing-room, wondering

what Jane would discover. But maybe I could make my own discoveries. These ladies might see more than they realized, if I could safely steer the conversation in the right direction.

Mary arrived with them, which sank my hopes for an enjoyable visit. It was hard to manage more than pleasantries, but I was grateful at least that John Reeves had not joined them.

It was not difficult to induce the ladies to speak of John.

"I am thoroughly tired of him!" Ghislaine declared.

"He is to be your husband," Mary said.

Ghislaine pouted. "My Papa desires it, but I think he only wishes me not to hinder him anymore in his adventures."

"Oh, you mustn't believe that!" Louisa said.

I leaned forward. "I don't know how it was in France, but in England, he cannot force you to marry someone you don't care for."

Ghislaine blinked hard. "Ah, but you don't know my Papa. Whatever he says, it becomes the truth. If he wished to be a...a king, he could make it so by speaking the words."

I repressed a smile at her faith in her father's ability.

"Well," Mary said. "Some ladies tell me my brother is considered a fine prospect for a husband—good enough even for a comte's daughter, I'm sure. Though I suppose if you're difficult to please, you would find a way to amuse yourself elsewhere."

Ghislaine sat upright. "You say that because I am French, but we are not all the same!"

Mary smirked at me. "Oh, it's not only the French who have immoral practices."

I watched her warily. "I suppose some Englishwomen also do such things."

She flicked her fan back and forth. "Oh, you pretend innocence, but I could tell you stories of Society!"

"Then I am glad I do not know much of Society."

"What of a harmless flirtation?" She raised her eyebrows. "Come, Lady Neale, I know our cousin the captain is in correspondence with you. I saw him writing something, and he said it was for you. Some people might say that looked suspicious."

I sat back, struggling not to gawk at her. She was accusing me of unfaithfulness? I could not let such rumors spread. "He was gathering memories of Eleanor for me. I am sorry I didn't have the opportunity to meet my husband's sister, and everything I can learn about her is precious."

Louisa and Ghislaine nodded sympathetically and launched into stories about Eleanor for my benefit. I tried to give them all my attention—both to know Eleanor better and to sift through the stories for clues—but Mary Reeves continued to smirk at me, and I suspected her gossiping tongue would mean trouble for me still.

CHAPTER 23

As soon as the Reeves sisters and Ghislaine left, I determined to tell Richard about the information Captain Reeves had gathered for me. Richard wouldn't like it, but I knew from bitter experience that rumors were like weeds: better to pull out the roots before they spread beyond control.

Richard was at the supper table once again that evening, and I brought Captain Reeves' list with me.

"What have you there? Another of my sister's stories?" He sounded hopeful.

"No." I set the papers down and lined up the edges. "This is information from the magistrate about the night she died."

He looked startled, and then his expression darkened. "And where did you acquire that?"

I sighed and met his accusing glare. "Captain Reeves."

"You involved him in this?"

"He is already involved, and he has access to information I could not get myself. If you could only learn to cooperate—"

Richard shook his head. "I want nothing to do with the captain. You should not be dealing with him either."

"I had to deal with someone when you would not even speak to me."

Richard's eyes hardened at that, every mask back in place. My heart ached at his renewed distance.

"Do you really think Captain Reeves killed your sister?" I asked more quietly.

Richard set his mouth in a stubborn line. "Perhaps not directly, but I think she was sneaking out to meet him when the villains who killed her set upon her. If it weren't for him, she would still be alive."

I saw the pain in his eyes. And the lie. Richard's argument over the captain had driven Eleanor to the garden.

I took his hand firmly. "The only person to blame is the one who killed her."

"How are you so certain it wasn't him?"

"I'm not positive, but I think it unlikely. I believe, like you, he would kill the fellow if he could. You could be allies."

He pulled his hand away. "Never!"

"You think he wasn't good enough for her. What, because of his background?"

"Not that. But he knew much of the world. She was innocent and full of dreams. She could not have made a fair judgement about his worthiness."

"How do you know he wasn't worthy of her?"

Richard's jaw worked, and he looked away. "Because he didn't protect her."

And with that, he stood and left the room, his supper turning cold on its abandoned plate.

I sank back in my chair, an ache pounding in my chest. I rested my face in my hands. In Richard's view, he had failed to protect Eleanor as well. I could not imagine the pain, but I knew Eleanor would not want either of them to carry such a burden of guilt. That was why I needed my answers.

I ate alone once again. I ought to be used to it, but after spending a couple of nights in Richard's company, the emptiness of the room filled my head and my heart, leaving me hollow. Richard might like the idea of offering me protection—perhaps making up for his supposed failure to protect his sister—but this would be no way to spend a lifetime.

To distract myself, I shuffled through the list of people who had been in attendance at the party. It was a long one, and it appeared that Captain Reeves had either taken the original papers or made a faithful copy. Many names were hastily crossed out, including all the women. I guessed perhaps they were accounted for at the time of the killing, or the elder Mr. Reeves thought them incapable of the crime.

The last page caught my eye. Someone had underlined one of the names. A dark splotch marred the paper beside it. I had to stare at it for some time to understand what I was seeing. Louis, Comte de Carriere. The comte had been at the party that night, and someone had put a mark by his name. What did it mean?

I had to show Richard, even if he wanted to avoid me.

I hurried through the house, but the corridors were

empty, the rooms dark. The only sound was my footsteps over the soft rugs.

I caught Harris near the kitchen. "Where is my husband?"

She gave me a suspicious look. "He went out."

"Oh, yes, naturally," I mumbled lamely.

Harris no doubt knew there was something off about our marriage. Her testimony would be useful when we had the marriage annulled. A wife would know when her husband was out.

He was out with his pistols and his mask—at least I knew one secret Harris did not. And one fear: On one of these rides, he was going to get himself killed.

With a sudden chill, I wondered if that was what he wanted. He blamed himself for Eleanor's death, and if he died trying to find her jewelry in the possession of the killer, he would consider it just. I had to find the killer first.

I couldn't ask the Reeves about their connection with the comte. He was their guest. They would not want to admit to harboring a killer. Though, it seemed strange that they would still harbor him if the elder Mr. Reeves suspected him.

But I knew someone besides the Reeves who would share neighborhood gossip with me. Also, someone who might give me a position when Richard grew weary of my presence. I had to make certain I had options. It was too late in the evening to go abroad, but in the morning, I would visit Mrs. Palmer and learn about the Comte de Carriere.

CHAPTER 24

It was a short walk to the Palmer's manor house the next morning. Their home was a squat, symmetrical Tudor building, not remodeled much over the centuries. Not large, but it looked comfortable enough.

Their footman seemed uncertain about what to do with a visitor. The Reeves must not call often. Given Mary Reeves' unkind comments about the Palmer's "sad" financial situation, the older couple might be glad to forgo their company. Mrs. Palmer must be lonely, though. That might mean she was more likely to hire a companion.

When the footman guided me inside, I couldn't help noticing the little signs that the Palmers did not have many financial resources. I knew the signs well because we had practiced the same economies as my father's gambling grew worse. Missing furniture and art. Linens mended many times over. More expensive repairs like rotted wood and leaky windows left undone and poorly hidden behind the remaining furnishings. The scents of cooking lingered in the air, but only bread and cabbage—no hint of roasted meat.

The Palmers were respectable and made a show of being comfortable, but that was the story they presented to the world. Here, I saw the reality. I wondered if I could send them some fish from Briarwood without injuring their pride. Mrs. Palmer might not be able to afford a companion after all. Though, perhaps I could help them with their economies and earn my keep that way. Anything to avoid being thrown back into Frances's clutches. Now that I had tasted freedom, I could not go back.

Mrs. Palmer seemed delighted to see me. We spoke briefly of mundane pleasantries, then she gave me a knowing look.

"I am enjoying your visit, but I do not flatter myself that young people enjoy visiting old ladies when they could be out with other persons their own age. Come, you know I am frank. Tell me what inspired your visit."

I smiled. "I do enjoy visiting with you, but I also hoped you could help me with some information."

"Ah." Mrs. Palmer sat back, a twinkle in her eyes. "Now we come to the heart of the matter. What can I tell you?"

"It's about Eleanor—Miss Neale. People do not like to speak of her, but I want to understand better."

Mrs. Palmer nodded. "Of course. The ghost of Briarwood."

I started and stared at her.

She smiled. "I do not mean a literal ghost, of course. But she haunts the place, doesn't she?"

I nodded, my mouth still dry.

"I still think of her as a child. We were friends with their parents, and we watched them grow up, brother and sister both. We never had children, you see."

I nodded, encouraging her to go on.

"Eleanor Neale was a delightful girl. Very lively and imaginative. Just listening to her made me feel more youthful." Mrs. Palmer's eyes brightened in the way everyone's seemed to when they thought of Eleanor. Then the brightness in them faded. "It is such a tragedy what happened to her."

"You don't think Richard did it," I said.

"No. That boy loved his sister. It's hard to imagine who might have wanted to harm her."

"Were you at the party?" I asked, though I knew she was from Mr. Reeves' list. Her name had been hastily crossed out.

She nodded sadly. "It was a lovely evening until the tragedy occurred. Everyone was in shock. No one could believe such a thing would happen."

"Did they search for a killer?"

"Oh, of course. They raced about in such chaos, it probably helped the villain escape."

"Hmm." Yes, if the killer was a member of the party, it would be easy to suddenly pretend to be a searcher. "Do you recall anyone acting suspiciously?"

She hesitated and pressed her lips together, her eyes filled with an uncertain memory. Then she sighed. "I don't know. Many people behaved in uncharacteristic ways, but it was such a shock, who knows how one is supposed to act?"

"Such as?" I pressed, convinced she knew something.

"Lord Neale argued with Captain Reeves, of course. I'm sure you've heard something of that."

"Had they been friendly before that night?"

"No, never. Lord Neale was always protective of his sister, though he'd never stooped to such an outright show of dislike as he did that night."

"Were the rest of the Reeves present?"

"Oh, yes. Those young ladies never miss a party. Miss Louisa crumpled when they announced the death. She fell to the floor screaming. It seemed very strange, but, again, most of us have never faced such a tragedy."

"And the rest of the Reeves?"

"Well, the elder Reeves was the magistrate, and we could see what a strain it was to do his duty, but he did. Of course, the inquest returned a verdict of homicide by person unknown."

"The comte was staying with the Reeves at the time, was he not?"

She tilted her head, her expression thoughtful. "In fact, he was. He and his daughter were at the party as well."

"They must have seen their share of violence before that night."

"No doubt. Ghislaine seemed deeply affected by her friend's death, but the comte looked fully indifferent."

"Did that seem strange to you?"

Mrs. Palmer gave me a sharp look. "Many things about the comte seem strange to me. There's a coldness beneath his show of charm. It was certainly unfeeling of him to react so shallowly, but I don't know if it was unusual for him."

"Yes, I see."

And I did. This did not mean that the comte was guilty, but he might be the type who could kill. Yet why would he want to?

"How does the comte know the Reeves?"

She wrinkled her forehead. "You know, I don't remember how they're acquainted. Perhaps Mr. Reeves met him on a visit to France before the troubles? The comte tells such wild stories, it's hard to know what's true and what's not."

"And the comte stays with him often?"

"Off and on. When he feels inclined to, it seems. I'm not sure the Reeves always welcome his long stays, but no one wants to be heartless to an emigre after all the troubles in France, especially if he is an old friend."

An old friend who could stay when and for as long as he wanted, and who could arrange an unwanted marriage between the only son of the family and his daughter. One whom the elder Reeves did not want to accuse, even if he suspected. There was something more to the story of the comte.

"Does the comte ever... Do you think he acts inappropriately toward young ladies?"

Mrs. Palmer raised her eyebrows. "An interesting question. I've heard nothing about that, but I am past an age to be trifled with, or to gossip with those who are. I would not put it past him, but I cannot say for certain."

"Was there anything else strange that night?" I asked.

Again, that uncertainty flickered in her eyes.

I leaned forward. "Anything you recall could help us find answers for poor Eleanor."

Mrs. Palmer sighed, her gaze hardened into determination. "No. Nothing I can remember would be helpful to you there, I'm afraid."

I didn't believe her, but I couldn't make her say more.

On my way out, I saw Mr. Palmer bent over one of the drains in the garden. I steered my steps in his direction, and he straightened at my approach, his expression wary. He glanced at his hands, dirty from labor. No longer the hands of a gentleman, despite what he tried to pretend for the world.

"Lady Neale." He executed a proper bow.

"Mr. Palmer. I hope you don't find this too strange, but I wondered if I could ask your opinion of the comte."

"The comte?" he looked confused.

"I have some concerns about him that I want to explore —discreetly, of course. I can easily ask the opinion of ladies, but aside from my husband, I don't have the opportunity to learn what experiences other gentlemen have of him."

"Experiences!" Mr. Palmer huffed. "You've seen the man. A self-important braggart."

"Do you think he could mean harm to anyone around him, though?"

Mr. Palmer hesitated over that, his bluster blown over. "I don't think he intends mischief, if that's what you mean. Rely on him only to look out for his best interests, though."

"I see. Do you remember his behavior at Eleanor Neale's ball last autumn?"

"The ball! That poor child." Mr. Palmer recoiled, then he shook his head, his whole face sagging into weary wrinkles. "That terrible night isn't one I want to relive—and you shouldn't either. Enjoy your youth and your health. When you're my age, you'll realize that sometimes it's better to let ghosts have their peace." He balled his hands into fists, the drying mud cracking along his knuckles, then let them hang limply at his side.

"Of course," I said. "Thank you for your time."

He nodded and trudged back to his labor. I turned for home, my thoughts full of the self-interested comte. Giving a ghost peace was exactly what I intended to do.

CHAPTER 25

Working in the garden helped me think, and I had a great deal to think about after my talk with Mrs. Palmer. Eleanor's roses had finally gone dormant for the winter, but I cleaned around them, knowing they would awaken again in the spring. I wondered if Richard would speak to me about the garden now, and I might ask him where his sister acquired her foreign flowers. But perhaps I had ruined all of our closeness by dealing with Captain Reeves. I sighed and tugged up another clump of grass crowding the roses.

"My lady!"

I looked up to see Jane hurrying toward me, her cheeks flushed red by the cool wind. Her eyes sparkled with news.

I sat on the bench and brushed off my skirt, my heart beating fast in anticipation.

"I found one of them," Jane panted, keeping her voice low. "One of the maids!"

"Oh! She's alive, then?"

"Yes, but frightened. She wouldn't say much to me—said that it was dangerous to talk. But she told me she left because of some papers."

"Papers?" I wrinkled my forehead. "Incriminating evidence, you mean?"

"Maybe. She only told me there were some papers she was supposed to find. When she couldn't find them, she was afraid someone would hurt her for it. She either didn't know who or was too scared to say."

It had to be Eleanor's writing. "What papers was she looking for, then? Stories?"

Jane sighed. "The girl can't read, unfortunately, so she didn't know what the papers said. She told me they would be sheets of paper with handwriting and something printed."

"Oh." I bit my lower lip, thinking. "What on earth could that be? Maybe something from a book?"

"I'm sorry I couldn't learn more," Jane said, looking defeated.

"Not at all! You did very well. Thank you."

Jane straightened her back like a soldier. "I'm not done yet, my lady. I'll find more girls. Maybe some of them who left the area will be more willing to talk. Maybe some will even know how to read and can tell me what the papers were supposed to say."

"Yes, we must find out."

Jane nodded. "Oh, and I thought I should warn you. Miss Louisa and Mademoiselle Carriere are having a picnic in the woods. You might not want to wander that way."

I hesitated. I was hesitant about Ghislaine now that I

suspected her father, but maybe this was my opportunity to find out more.

"Thank you for the warning," I said, "but it might be useful to speak to them again."

Jane looked skeptical at that, but she shrugged and went back to her work in the house.

I sighed and straightened my dress, picking a stray leaf from my skirt. I had my own work to do.

I wandered down to the woods, following well-worn trails through the tangle of old trees. It wasn't long before I heard the sounds of female voices. At least it was only Louisa and Ghislaine. I wanted no more of Mary's gossip.

"Good morning!" I called out.

"Oh, Lady Neale, is that you?" Louisa said. "We are over here, having a picnic. Do join us."

I found them in a clearing in the woods, settled with baskets full of fresh-picked blackberries—no doubt the briars that gave Richard's home its name.

"You must enjoy them while you can," Ghislaine prompted. "Soon it will freeze, and we will not see them for another year."

"It must have been a sad day at Briarwood yesterday," Louisa said.

I paused with a blackberry halfway to my mouth. Had rumors spread of my disagreement with Richard?

"The anniversary of the...the ball," Louisa finished.

"Oh, yes." November was fast dwindling, and Eleanor had wanted her ball to be the first winter celebration. I swallowed the blackberry without tasting it.

Richard hadn't said anything about the day. Of course he

hadn't. I was only a temporary guest. It had been an especially bad day to bring up Captain Reeves and the list of party guests, though. Guilt stabbed through me.

Ghislaine sighed. "Yes, and we decided today we must be out of the house. Mary and John were exceedingly vexing, especially to poor Louisa."

Louisa pressed her lips together. "You should not marry John. I know I wouldn't want to be his wife!"

"Yes, but you are spared the problem by being his sister," Ghislaine said. "Though it also means you can't escape him. Ah, perhaps Papa will change his mind. His does become restless at times."

"He seems to genuinely care for you," I said, seizing the opportunity to speak of the comte.

Ghislaine stared at the purple-stained tips of her fingers. "Some of the time. At others, he only cares for himself. Then I feel like only a pretty ornament to him—one he tires of showing off. It must be very inconvenient to have a silly girl to care for all the time, and I do not wish to be a burden any longer."

My chest ached for her. Ghislaine was a sweet girl—very lovely—and if she might be a bit silly, that did not make her a burden. Yet how often had I felt inconvenient, no matter how useful I tried to be? As if my very existence—my lack of beauty and charm—was a problem for everyone around me that I had to amend. Yet I had held the household together until Father's death shattered it. And then I had scrambled to pick up the pieces. How could I have been the burden when I carried so much on my shoulders?

I grasped Ghislaine's hand. "If your father sees you that

way, it is his failing, not yours. No parent should make their child feel such."

My words sounded back to me and settled, warm around my heart.

Ghislaine smiled sadly. "You are most kind."

We returned our attention to the blackberries, commenting on the weather and the views. Exceedingly polite and exceedingly unhelpful. Perhaps this was why Richard took to highway robbery instead. It was certainly more direct. But that gave me an idea.

"Ghislaine, what a lovely necklace," I said, gesturing to the little cross she wore.

"Oh, thank you! It was one I was able to bring from France."

"You must have left much behind."

Ghislaine laughed. "Oh, you do not know my papa! He always manages to come out on top of the situation."

"He is very charming. He must have ladies eating out of his hand."

Ghislaine rolled her eyes. "Oh, there are always women who flirt with him, but he holds himself aloof. He is not so French as all that."

A jolt raced through me. The comte was not French?

Ghislaine's eyes widened slightly, and she said, "Pardon my poor English. What I mean is that not all Frenchmen are like the stories you hear."

"Oh, of course," I said, but there was nothing wrong with Ghislaine's English. In fact, it was surprisingly good for a girl who had never been in England before the Revolution.

I quickly steered the conversation to safer ground,

pretending to have forgotten all about the slip, but I turned it over and over in my mind. I didn't know what secrets the comte was hiding, but I was convinced he was not what he seemed. Would he threaten maids to steal evidence of his true identity? Would he kill to keep his secret?

I made my excuses and headed back to Briarwood, holding my skirts so they did not snag on brambles as I hurried. I spotted Richard coming from the stables and ran to catch up with him. His hair was tousled by his ride—and no doubt by the mask he had worn—and I repressed an urge to reach out and straighten it.

He gave me a curt nod, and his coldness sent a chill through me. But I had to be practical and forget our disagreement—and whatever had been happening between us before the disagreement—in pursuit of answers for Eleanor.

"My lord,' I said, not daring to the informality of using his Christian name.

He scowled, his expression guarded.

"Any success?" I asked.

"None."

"I might have found something," I said.

He raised an eyebrow, waiting.

"What do you know of the Comte de Carriere?"

"He is a friend of the Reeves' and a pompous peacock."

"*Is* he their friend, though?"

He considered that, and his indifference slipped. "No, I don't think so. They don't seem to enjoy his company, only tolerate it. I suppose they feel some obligation to help him."

"I don't think he's what he seems. Ghislaine said something today that makes me suspect they are not actually French."

"Really?" His expression turned thoughtful. "There are some adventurers who take advantage of the chaos on the continent to pass themselves off as aristocrats deserving of sympathy. I believe him capable of it."

"Did he ever show any interest in your sister? Or she in him?"

"None in particular. She liked stories, so she was interested in his, but they had little interaction beyond formal social occasions."

"If she discovered something about him, though—something in his stories that didn't add up—might he have threatened her to keep her quiet?"

His eyes darkened. "It's not impossible, though it would be very risky for him to do such a thing. He's more likely to be uncovered by committing murder than by a young lady gossiping..."

"But?" I pressed.

He sighed. "It's not impossible."

"Do you remember him being there that night?"

His face tightened. "Yes, he was there. He likes the spotlight, so he was in the ballroom."

"The entire time?"

He rubbed his eyes. "I can't be certain."

"His name was on the...the list. It was not crossed out. In fact, it was underlined and marked. Yet Mr. Reeves said nothing about whatever suspicions he had. If the comte had some power over the Reeves, some threat that he's exploiting, he might be guilty of worse crimes." Threatening maids

—who couldn't read the papers and discover his secret. Murder. Another thought fell into place. "He was in Bath, too, when the man was killed in the garden."

Richard set his jaw. "I see." His face softened a little as he looked down at me. "Thank you for telling me."

Then he strode off at such a pace that I would not be able to keep up with him. I had helped. I may have even found the key, and soon, Eleanor's killer would face justice. Then why did I feel defeat instead of triumph?

CHAPTER 26

Richard was not at the supper table that evening, nor anywhere in the house. He must have gone to confront the comte. I paced the corridors as dark gathered outside, as restless as any ghost. Eleanor did not appear to keep me company. Did that mean we'd found our answer? If so, my charade as Lady Neale was over. I stopped in front of the ballroom where Richard had taught me to waltz. The dancing figures on the ceiling continued their capering, heedless of me. Something inside me twisted, and I whirled away.

The library. At least I could go there one more time. The scent of leather and ink greeted me. I couldn't focus on a novel, so I searched through more of Eleanor's stories, looking for any that had printing on them. Any that might confirm my suspicions about the comte or reveal what power he held over the Reeves.

A tap on the door sent my heart racing. It must be Richard. I pulled the door open.

Harris stood on the threshold, her face pale. Angry at finding me in the library? No, afraid.

Richard?

I gripped the door frame. "What's happened?"

She clasped and unclasped her hands. "It's... You have guests, my lady."

I drew a slow breath. The kind of guests who asked questions about highwaymen, perhaps? "Who is it?"

"It's a gentleman who claims to be your brother."

It took a moment for the words to make sense. "Julian?"

"He gave his name as Mr. Ratliffe. But...my lord is away from home."

My shoulders relaxed. She might have instructions to turn guests away—especially guests arriving at odd hours— but I felt equal to handling my brother. "I will deal with Mr. Ratliffe. Thank you, Harris."

She still looked nervous but led me back to the drawing-room. Julian sat there, fidgeting with his gloves, while Frances sprawled out on the sofa with a handkerchief clutched to her nose.

"Athena!" Julian jumped to his feet and rushed to embrace me. "You look well."

"Thank you," I said, though I could not return the compliment. Frances appeared quite miserable, and we both glanced at her.

"Um, yes." Julian apologized with his eyes. "I'm afraid Frances has taken sick and couldn't travel any further."

"With the Advent season nearly upon us," Frances sniffled, "I knew you would not turn us away."

"I'm sorry," Julian mouthed.

I forced a smile, though my lips felt trembly. "No, we cannot turn you away."

But what a mess this was! Frances might be truly ill, or she might simply wish to spend her Christmas in the home of a baron. She had no idea what a bee's nest she was really stumbling into.

"I will find you a room to rest," I said to them both. "But please understand, my husband is only just out of mourning, and we did not plan large festivities this Christmas."

"Oh, you need not do anything extravagant for us, I'm sure," Frances cooed.

I nodded slowly. I could explain Christmas away, but we were short on servants, and of course we were involved in activities they could not know about. And Richard still had not returned. Maybe he had seen Julian and Frances on the road and hoped to avoid them.

The best thing to do would be to have them settled in a far corner of the house where they would not see or be seen. I found Harris still hovering behind me.

"Make up a guest room for them, Harris. The one with the Hades and Persephone painting ought to be suitable."

She nodded and left with swift dignity.

"We must get you settled," I told Frances. "You have your maid with you?"

"Only my lady's maid."

"And my valet," Julian added. "We sent all the others ahead of us."

I nodded. That might be for the best, since fewer strangers meant fewer people to hide things from.

"Briarwood can accommodate you, though I have not yet finished hiring a full staff."

Frances harrumphed and gave me a look that showed how much she thought I was lacking. I turned away so she would not see anything more from me, and I had to see no more from her.

"Thank you," Julian said in a low tone. "And I am glad to see you, and that you look happy."

"Of course," I said, and my chest warmed at his words. It was good to see him as well, if strange having my two worlds collide. "Let's help Frances to her chamber."

Once we had Frances settled, after much rearranging to suit her nerves, I excused myself. I did want to visit with Julian, and hated to leave him alone with his repining wife, but I needed time to gather my thoughts and my emotions.

Jane found me in my chamber. She swept inside and shut the door behind her.

"Frances is here?" she whispered, her eyes wide.

"Unfortunately, yes. I suppose a visit was inevitable." At least, since we didn't annul the marriage quickly enough.

"Will she stay long?"

My shoulders slumped. "She claims to be quite ill and looking forward to a peaceful Christmas season."

Jane groaned. Then her expression brightened. "At least you have the satisfaction of showing her your success."

"Oh, yes." I could not make myself sound enthusiastic.

"My lady?"

She was being impertinent, and I could send her off on

some errand, but I was swirling with emotions that needed an outlet, even if it wasn't all the truth.

"She reminds me of my mother," I said.

Jane's eyes widened. "Your mother? Frances is nothing like your mother!"

"They at least share in their disapproval of me."

"Disapproval? When did your mother ever disapprove of you?"

Jane was a couple of years older than me, so she would have remembered my mother, but I doubted she saw everything I did.

I spun the ring on my finger. "Oh, just that I was not as lovely and refined as she was."

"You are dark where she was fair, but otherwise, you look almost identical. I can't imagine her saying such unkind things. She was always sweet-natured. If anything, I wish she had been a little firmer. Especially with that governess Miss Davidson."

"Miss Davidson?" The name left a bad taste in my mouth. Her voice was always in my head, but I had not spoken of her for years. "What do you mean?"

Jane looked at me in surprise, then her face softened. "Oh, I suppose you wouldn't have known. Your mother always wanted to dote on you, but that awful governess told her she would spoil you and make you vain, pretty thing that you were."

"But..." My head swam at this information. My mother had wanted to visit me? Had thought I was pretty? "But when I snuck into the ball she was so upset. Ashamed of me."

"I remember that night," Jane said firmly. "She was ashamed of herself. Upset because she believed your spirited actions showed she was a bad mother to you, guiding you to vanity and vice. I heard her tell your father that you looked so lovely and hopeful that she wished you could have stayed and danced. But Miss Davidson stepped in and told them they were being too soft."

I sat heavily, almost missing the chair. "She wanted me there?"

Jane nodded firmly. "Never doubt it. My mother said that governess and her nasty words were a poison in your family, but Miss Davidson had worked for a noble family and came with high recommendations, so your parents thought they were helping you to be better through her."

I let out a heavy breath and turned to stare into my dressing table mirror. My mother had loved me? She thought me pretty and wanted me close? I tightened my fist, feeling my mother's ring press into my skin. If only I had known! If only none of us had listened to Miss Davidson.

"Thank you for telling me," I whispered.

Jane scooted closer. "If I had realized you didn't know, I would have told you sooner. We always hoped to see you bloom despite your mother's loss and that woman's efforts to clip every flower you produced."

"Oh," I said, my throat tight.

I stared in the mirror, trying to see myself anew. Trying to see a pretty girl whose mother loved her. My reflection stared back at me, full of uncertainty. And perhaps also hope.

CHAPTER 27

I could not fall asleep that night. I lay on my back and rethought my childhood. Then tossed to my right and worried about Richard. I rolled over again and found myself trying to decide what to do about Julian and Frances.

A crash from downstairs roused me. I pulled my blanket close, and my pulse thundered. Had the intruder returned? And Richard was still gone. Julian might help this time, though I hated the idea of him being injured because of my problems.

I threw on my dressing robe and snuck down the stairs, a candlestick my only weapon. The brass was cold in my grip. I would have to find out where Richard kept his spare pistols if he was going to leave me unprotected.

But it was Richard in the front hall, leaning heavily on Walters. He was pale. Blood dripped to the floor from his red-stained sleeve.

I dropped the candlestick, and it clattered, the little flame snuffed on the wool rug. "Richard!"

He looked up at me with eyes going glassy. "Oh. You were right about the danger. I suppose you'll be pleased."

"Don't be ridiculous! I don't want you shot."

My mind flew everywhere in a panic, but I forced it to settle on Richard. I had dealt with father's injuries when a bout of gambling with unsavory fellows had gone badly for him. I turned on Walters.

"Tell me what happened. Did the comte do this?"

The man swallowed, his Adam's apple bouncing. "No, it happened on the road. The man in the carriage drew a pistol on him. He's hit in the shoulder."

I sighed. "It could be worse, then."

"The ball is still lodged in there, my lady. I could not get him to hold still long enough to dig it free."

"It will have to come out," I said. "Take him to his chambers and bring me the strongest brandy we have. Oh, and try not to be noisy—my brother and his wife are here."

Walters grimaced at that, and Richard looked at me in dazed confusion. But we managed to get Richard up the stairs and into his antechamber.

Walters left Richard on the sofa and hurried off. I turned to my husband.

"I suppose you'll be rid of me now," he said.

"Hardly. If you'll stop being so dramatic, we'll get the ball out and you'll recover."

"They'll be looking for an injured man."

I went cold at the thought, but I didn't let it show. "Then

it's a good thing that you're so reclusive. We'll have you better before anyone notices."

"It's going to take a fierce amount of brandy to keep me still enough to dig that ball out. I think it's in the bone."

"All the more reason we have to remove it."

I put on a brave face, but my stomach felt like I had swallowed a rock. This was a serious injury. It didn't kill him outright, but the infection might.

A loud pounding sounded from the front door.

"That will be the hue and cry," Richard slurred. "They'll want me to come out and search with them. They'll know it was me when I can't."

"I'll delay them," I said.

I hurried to the front door, scrambling in my mind for what to say to the constable.

I swung the door open. Captain Reeves was there. Was Captain Reeves a constable? Perhaps.

"Where is your husband?" Captain Reeves asked.

"He's attending his favorite horse. It injured a hock and may not survive."

Captain Reeves smiled. "Clever excuse, but I was walking the pond by moonlight and saw his valet drag him, injured, into the house."

I hesitated. I trusted Captain Reeves. Mostly. But this was a far heavier secret than asking him to help me find a murderer.

Captain Reeves clasped my arm. "For Eleanor's sake, I don't want him to die. I've been in battle. I can treat wounds. And I can keep secrets."

I glanced back to the stairs. "Very well. Come in."

Richard looked up when we entered the room. He struggled to sit up. "What is he doing here? He is forbidden from entering this house."

I stepped between Richard and the captain. "He's here to help save your life. You're going to need someone to dig that ball out of your shoulder, and I don't know how."

"No! I won't allow him to cut into me."

I folded my arms. "Then we will just wait until you pass out from the blood loss and do it then."

Walters returned with the brandy.

"Give it to me," Richard growled.

Walters went for a glass, but Richard shook his head. "Just give me the bottle."

"We'll need some for cleaning, too," Captain Reeves said with a thin smile.

Richard took a swig from the bottle and leaned his head back. "Do what you must."

The captain nodded. "We'll need a clean cloth and good light. Bring the lamp closer. Get me some hot water and some tweezers."

Walters ran about at his commands.

Captain Reeves looked to the valet. "Hold him down. No matter what he says or does."

I swallowed. This was going to be brutal.

"You can leave," the captain told me.

"No, I'm going to stay. I'll help."

It was going to be ugly, but I was not leaving Richard alone.

Walters held Richard down, I held the light, and Captain Reeves dug the ball out of Richard's shoulder. There was a great deal of blood, but Richard did not scream, and I did not pass out. Richard didn't pass out, either, but he was dazed by the end.

Captain Reeves beckoned me aside. "You'll have to keep it clean. The risk of infection is high, but if he makes it through the next week, he should survive."

I nodded, feeling light-headed.

A knock sounded on the front door, echoing through the house.

"Who will that be?" I asked.

Captain Reeves frowned. "It may be the constable. Whatever caused your husband's misadventure, word will get around quickly that there was a violent incident."

I clasped my clammy hands. "What will tell him?"

"I assume you can't tell the truth?" the captain asked.

I shook my head. "He can't know that Richard was shot tonight."

"Hmm. I think I can help." Captain Reeves smiled grimly and went to the door.

I lingered on the stairs so I could listen out of sight.

Captain Reeves opened the door. "Constable! Oh, this is unfortunate."

"Unfortunate! What are you doing here, Captain Reeves? Is Lord Neale having a house party?"

Could that excuse work? Probably not.

"Oh, a party of sorts," the captain said.

"There's blood on your clothes!" the constable said. "What devilry is this?"

"You have found us out. I'm afraid Lord Neale and I have

had a difficult disagreement. A gentleman's reckoning, if you will."

"Dueling!" the constable cried.

"Oh, let's not use that term. It's unsavory, and we both have reputations to protect. Plus, there is the question of the, er, source of our disagreement."

"Do you have any seconds who can verify this claim? We're on the hunt for a criminal—two criminals, in fact—and the timing of this is very suspicious."

I walked down the stairs, prepared to perjure myself, though no one would believe I had been a second at a duel.

"There is Richard's valet," I offered.

The constable looked skeptical. A valet was not a reliable witness for his own master.

"I can vouch for them," my brother said from the top of the stairs. He bounded down and stood before the constable. "Julian Ratliffe. Lady Neale's brother. I'm visiting here, and I witnessed the whole thing."

He gave me a significant look. Oh, dear.

The constable looked between all of us. "You're willing to swear to it?"

"Of course," Julian said.

The constable relaxed. "I'm glad to hear it. I did not look forward to the scandal this would cause." He gave Captain Reeves a sad look. "Miss Neale always did come between you two. Even now that she's gone, I suppose."

The captain cleared his throat. "I would prefer her name did not come up in the discussion. You understand, of course. Gentleman to gentleman."

"Ah, of course, Captain. Normally, I would have something to say about this matter... No one was killed, I take it."

"Lord Neale came out the worse between the two of us, but I'm hopeful for his survival."

"Well, I'll let this go for now, then. I'm on the hunt for a highwayman."

"I would help, but I feel obligated to assist his lordship in cleaning up," Captain Reeves said.

"Of course."

The constable retreated into the dark.

Captain Reeves closed the door with a sigh. "Well, I certainly hope Lord Neale does not die, because if he does, I'll have to flee the country." He glanced at Julian. "I'd better go see how my lord is faring."

I turned to Julian with no idea what to say.

He shook his head. "Athena, I don't know, and I don't want to know."

"You said—"

"I only heard bits and pieces. Enough to know you were in trouble. And I have so many black marks by my name, a little lie didn't seem to do much harm, especially not in the interest of protecting my sister."

I threw my arms around him. "Thank you!"

He returned the embrace. "We need never speak of it again. Only, stay safe, and if I can help in any way..."

I released him and shook my head. "I hope you will not need to. I hope the trouble is over. But thank you."

I hurried back to Richard's room to find him finally unconscious.

"I'm sorry I can't do more," Captain Reeves said, watching Richard with a frown. "For Eleanor's sake."

"You have saved us. Thank you."

He nodded and wiped his hands clean, then glanced back to the corridor. "It's strange. As I was working, I almost felt like she was standing beside me."

"I think perhaps she was. She is grateful, too."

He swallowed and nodded, his eyes full of sorrow. "Good night, Lady Neale. I will mention my exploits at home, and cousin Mary will be certain everyone knows about the duel."

He smiled a little at that, bowed, and left.

I turned to Walters, who shifted from foot to foot like a schoolboy caught stealing from the kitchen.

"I told him he was getting too reckless," the valet said.

I sighed. "I'm certain you did what you could to protect him. Did he not try to investigate the Comte de Carriere?" Had he not taken me seriously, after all the effort I made?

"Oh, he tried, but the comte wasn't at home. My lord fretted that he would not be able to prove his case or that the villain would escape. And...and he agonized knowing even the most perfect justice won't bring back Miss Neale. He grew impatient and decided to accost the first carriage that passed our way. It was almost like he wanted to be caught."

I nodded. It was what I had feared. "You need to wash up and rest. I will watch Richard tonight."

CHAPTER 28

The next few days blurred into a haze of exhaustion and worry. Thanks to the story of the duel, we were able to bring in a doctor, but Richard sank into a fever. The doctor instructed us to clean his wound often and give him teas of willow bark.

"Beyond that, I'm afraid there's nothing to be done but hope his body purges the infection," the doctor warned. "He has to fight it."

I nodded numbly. But Richard had courted trouble. Had sought the punishment he thought he deserved for failing his sister. How to call him back now?

Frances hobbled down the corridor to order the doctor to attend to her cold, her voice cutting into the ache behind my eyes. Were it not for my love of Julian, I would have thrown her from the house.

Walters and I took turns caring for Richard while Harris kept us well-supplied with healing teas.

Richard mumbled in his feverish sleep. "Protect her. Must protect her."

"Eleanor is safe," I lied, trying to calm his agitated mind.

"Athena."

"Yes, I'm here."

"Keep her safe. Athena. Oh, Athena. Please. Don't leave."

His words sent a thrill through me. He wanted me there. Or, he wanted me to avenge Eleanor, at least. Because didn't think he would live?

"I'm sorry," he whispered.

I grasped his hand, but he said no more.

I tried to keep him clean and comfortable, but it wasn't enough—I wasn't doing enough. He drifted out of awareness, and his skin was hot to the touch. He no longer tossed or groaned, only lay deathly still on the bed.

"You have to fight—for Eleanor's sake," I whispered to him again and again, my voice hoarse.

He showed no signs of hearing.

I wanted to beg him for my own sake, but what would be the purpose in it? He wasn't mine, and he never would be. A deep, weary ache settled inside me, not even eased when I took my turn sleeping.

I sat bathing Richard's forehead after a long night gave way to a weak, gray dawn. Harris brought fresh water and tea along with a letter.

"From the Reeves," she said grimly.

I braced myself for whatever they might say. I hoped they were not throwing Captain Reeves out of the house. He had put his life on the line by lying for us, especially if Richard didn't recover. If...if the worst happened, I had already decided to tell the truth about Richard's injury. I thought he would prefer more scandal instead of the ruin of another man's life.

I pressed my lips together, my tired eyes watering. I would not have to make that decision. Richard *would* recover.

I opened the note find an invitation from Mary Reeves to take tea with her. 'In the interest of maintaining goodwill between our families.'

"Really!" I huffed.

I turned back to carefully clean Richard's wound. The skin was an angry red, and even in his unconsciousness, Richard winced at my careful touch.

"She is probably only looking for more gossip," I told him.

I paused. This might present an opportunity. I needed proof that the comte was a fraud. If I could find justice for Eleanor, maybe that news would reach Richard, and he wouldn't give up.

Walters came in to take his turn at his master's bedside. "You'd best sleep while you can, my lady. He wouldn't want you to run yourself down."

"Thank you, Walters," I said.

But I had another scheme in mind. Jane echoed Walters' concerns over my exhaustion, but she helped me dress and try to look presentable. Deep circles under my eyes stood out against my pale skin, but fortunately, I never put any store in being pretty. My obvious weariness might even garner me some sympathy and aid my search.

Jane helped me into my fine, white muslin gown like a squire dressing his knight for battle, and I went to face

Mary Reeves—and hopefully the so-called Comte de Carriere.

"I do hope Lord Neale is recovering well," Mary said once we were settled with our tea. "Papa is furious with the captain."

"He should not be," I said quickly. "Do you not think my husband equally guilty?"

If they threw Captain Reeves out of the house, I would invite him to stay with us, but that would not stop the gossip or please my husband. If he became conscious enough to learn of it.

Mary shrugged. "Even if he is, my Papa can only have any say over the captain, and he's already unhappy with all of his long-term guests."

Here was my opportunity. "Oh? I would think the comte, at least, would add some interest to your parties."

She rolled her eyes. "At first, I suppose. But we have heard enough of his wild tales, and he is very demanding. He takes the best rooms, the best foods, and Papa does whatever he asks. Honestly, I'm not certain why he tolerates him except that no one wants to be thought ungenerous."

"They are old friends, are they not?"

She wrinkled her forehead and placed her cup down with a gentle *tink*. "That is what they say, but I never heard Papa mention him until he suddenly arrived one day. I suppose maybe he was a friend who Papa forgot. Or wanted to forget," she added meaningfully.

I mulled that over while the string of gossip continued. The comte had some hold over the Reeves. I just had to know what.

As we finished our visit, I invented an excuse to linger. "Louisa told me that you might have some of Eleanor's favorite books in your library."

"Do we?" Mary sounded bored. "I wouldn't know. I never go in there. Just look what they do to Louisa—fill her weak brain with silly ideas."

I took a deep breath and forced a polite smile. "May I look before I leave? I will return any that I borrow."

Mary waved her hand dismissively. "That's not how I would spend *my* time, but feel free to take them away."

"Thank you," I said serenely, but my pulse hammered in my throat. Here was my chance.

Mary guided me to the library. As I lingered over the books, she quickly grew bored and left me to "enjoy myself as long as I liked."

Once I was certain she was gone, I snuck out of the library and down the corridor. Thanks to my misadventures at the dinner party, I knew which way the guest quarters lay. I even knew where Ghislaine's room was, and I doubted her father was too far from her.

I listened at the doors, and then tested one. Unoccupied, the furnishings covered in sheets. The next one, also. Miss Reeves had said the comte had the finest guest room. That one with the largest door must be it.

Once again, I listened at the door and heard no sound from within. I tried the handle. Locked. Hmm. The comte guarded his secrets. That was a problem.

Ah, but I had seen the servants' door in the library. I was willing to wager that he had not blocked the servants' access to his room. I hurried back to the servants' entrance and snuck down the narrow corridor, counting doors until I came to the comte's room.

The door swung open, and I slipped inside.

The room was dim, the curtains drawn over the window, and I took a moment to make certain I was truly alone. The quiet rang in my ears, and I took a deep breath. Time to unmask the comte. I rummaged through trunks and drawers looking for some hint of his hold over the Reeves or his fixation with Eleanor.

It looked like he burned most of his letters. Ashy scraps of paper clung to the fireplace grate. In one drawer, I found a few legal documents. One looked familiar. Eleanor had a similar paper in her desk. I studied it. Shares in the East India Company. Five thousand pounds worth—a small fortune. But they weren't the comte's. They belonged to a Hugh Reeves. The other documents in the drawer also bore the name of Hugh Reeves. Was that the elder Mr. Reeves' Christian name? Or the captain's father? Had the comte stolen the Reeves' documents? Why?

A small, enameled box tucked out of sight in the back of a closet caught my eye. I carefully opened it and found a family seal ring inside. Odd. If anything, this proved that he was of noble or at least honorable birth. I looked more closely at the seal ring.

It bore the crest of the Reeves family. I felt the weight of it in my hand, trying to decipher what this meant. Had he stolen it? It didn't have any value to a thief; he wouldn't be able to use it for anything except perhaps to impersonate the elder Mr. Reeves in business dealings. And if he was forcing the Reeves to do his bidding, he didn't need the ring; he only had to threaten them with whatever secret he held, and they would use it for him.

Why would he keep the ring?

I frowned and put it on my finger. It was much too large, of course. It would be fitted to its owner.

Its owner—the scion of the Reeves family.

A shock ran through me, raising the hairs on my arms.

That was it. The "comte" would keep the ring if it was his. If he was the eldest Reeves black sheep, the one long ago absconded to France. Eleanor had written a story about a prodigal son returning to bleed his family dry. My heartbeat pulsing in my ears. The ring proved he was the heir. However disreputable he might be, he could claim the Reeves' estate, their wealth, and the place as the local squire, even throw them out if he wished.

He was Hugh Reeves.

Then why not reveal himself?

I thought of Ghislaine's stories, and Eleanor's, and the pieces fell into place.

He didn't want to. He liked the life he led, carefree and acclaimed everywhere he went. And the Reeves had to support him because he could take everything from them.

That might be a secret worth killing over.

I shoved the ring back in its box and hid it again. I knew the secret, but what to do about it?

I rushed for the servants' entrance, but even as I reached for the handle, the narrow door swung open. My chest constricted, and I scrambled for an excuse for being caught in the comte's room by one of the servants. Could I bribe them to stay quiet?

But it wasn't a servant who slipped through the door. It was the comte.

We stared at each other in shock.

"You are not one of the servants," he said.

"No. I was playing a game with Louisa, and I lost my way."

He studied me for a moment, then a glint shone in his eyes. "Or perhaps you were looking for me?"

Oh no, no, no.

"Absolutely not!" I backed away, my stomach churning.

I had to dart past him to the servants' door or unlock the main door to the corridor to make my escape. Could I do either without him grabbing me?

"No need to be shy. I know many women find me irresistible."

Anger flashed through me at his cocky smirk. "Is that what you thought about Eleanor Neale?"

His smile faded. "That child that was killed? Bah, I have no interest in little maidens."

"You're lying. I know your secret!"

He raised his quizzing glass. I did not flinch from his gaze. After all, I knew that he was no comte. He was only a country squire, and I was the wife of a baron.

"What an interesting creature you are," he said, not dropping his accent. "Isn't it more usual, when one discovers a dastardly secret, to use it for leverage? Ah! Or, perhaps *that* is why you're here? How dramatic."

"Is that what you thought of Eleanor? That she would threaten you?"

He frowned and tapped his quizzing glass against his

lower lip. Then his eyes brightened, and he chuckled. "Oh, you think I killed her? Why would I bother?"

"She knew you are no Comte de Carriere. You are plain Hugh Reeves!"

He raised his chin. "I have never been plain. I was once Hugh Reeves, but now I am Carriere. It is who I choose to be. Whatever I say is the truth."

"And Eleanor dared to question your delusion."

He shook his head. "Ask yourself, Lady Neale, what would have happened if she convinced others that I am Reeves?"

I fumbled over that. "Society would stop fawning over you. You would hate that."

"You think they would fawn less? A rich and vanished heir returned from harrowing adventures abroad? The gossips would love it. I would turn it to my advantage. I always do. That is why I do not fear threats."

My hands felt cold and stiff. I believed him. He was just mad enough to be telling the truth.

He smiled at me—not the smile of a wolf, but a clever fox. "If you are looking for threats, you must look elsewhere. Or, you could stay, and we could discuss it further? It might be amusing." He stepped closer. Too close.

"No. We have no business together."

And on that, I fled the room and the house.

CHAPTER 29

My head spun with exhaustion and confusion as I stumbled home from the Reeves.' Everything inside me felt hollowed out. I wanted to cry, but my eyes were too tired and numb. I had nothing left. Richard was feverish, perhaps dying. I couldn't help him, and I couldn't help Eleanor.

At Briarwood, I retreated to my room and sank into a restless sleep full of prowling wolves.

When I ventured out of my room again, evening light filtered into the corridors. Julian was there, wandering from portrait to portrait in a restless pacing.

"Athena!" He hurried over to me.

"Is Frances worse?" I asked dully. There was probably nothing I could do for her either.

"She'll recover soon enough," Julian said.

"Any change with Richard?" I asked, my voice tight.

"Nothing that I've heard."

I nodded, hardly seeing Julian or anything around us.

"I was concerned about you," Julian said.

"Me?" I looked at him in surprise. "I am not injured."

"No, but you are wearing yourself down. Worrying. I can see it."

"Of course I'm worrying! I'm helpless and useless, and I don't know what to do."

"You are never useless! You were always the one who held everything together..." Something flickered in Julian's eyes. "We always required you to keep everything together, didn't we? Once mother was gone. Father was drowning his sorrows and I was hiding from him and from myself, and we left you to pick everything up and carry on. I'm so sorry, Athena."

I stared at him, confused by his apology. "That's what I was there for," I mumbled. "I'm the practical one."

"Perhaps you are, but you're more than that. Frances manages the household quite effectively, but there is a light missing from it without you there. You were not born simply to...to be a drudge! I remember how Mother doted on you. And you seemed such a happy child, running in the gardens almost as soon as you had your feet under you. You brought smiles to all of us. I wish I had been there more to remind you."

"Remind me?"

Julian took my hands. "Athena, you were born for joy."

The words filled me with warmth, even as I struggled to understand them. "Our life has not been a happy one."

"No, and no one can expect to always be happy. But there is a light in you. We stuffed it under a bushel—your priggish governess and then father and...and I as well—and I've watched you grow dimmer. I would see that light shine again, sister."

"I'm...I'm not sure that's still me." But Richard had thanked me for bringing light back to Briarwood. Maybe they saw something I did not. "I will try to find that light again—if you will promise to do the same."

Julian looked like he might object, but then he caught himself. "You are right. I have resigned myself to gloom as well. Father's choices left a long shadow over us, but we are not him. We can step out from that shadow for ourselves, even if Society does not like it."

I embraced him. "Thank you, Julian."

He returned the embrace awkwardly, patting me on the back.

I left him and went to check on Richard. Sleeping—he and Walters both. Richard's forehead was still too warm, but perhaps not quite as hot as before. I reached a tentative hand to stroke the dark stubble covering his cheek.

"Please get well," I whispered.

His eyes fluttered, and he looked at me through glassy eyes. "Don't leave me," he rasped. "I cannot bear it."

My heart lurched. Did he think I was Eleanor? "I'm still here."

He fumbled out with his hand, and I took it.

He drifted back to sleep, and I lowered his hand, reluctant to let it go. I had grown to like being his wife. I even liked the idea of being his real wife. But I wasn't sure he'd ever put his mask aside completely. Maybe once we had answers about Eleanor.

If he wouldn't, though...

I thought of what Julian had said, and I studied Richard's face. I might never find love—that was something I could not control—but maybe there *could* be light and joy in my life. I had believed the stories Miss Davidson had told me, but they weren't true. Jane, Richard, and Julian all told me different stories—better ones. A quiet whisper in my heart did as well. I still thought the so-called comte was mad, believing whatever he said was truth, but perhaps he was right in one thing: the stories we told ourselves mattered.

I kissed Richard's hand and left him, returning to the library. I shut the door, put my back to it, and scanned the room. There was something here. Something Eleanor wanted me to find. An answer.

I sat and sorted through more of her papers, flipping through stories and even some sketches. All little pieces of the story, but none of them complete.

"What is here that someone would kill you over?" I whispered. "What do you want to tell me?"

The papers in my lap slid to the floor. I scrambled to pick them up. As I did, a paper caught my eye. Shares in the East India Company, just like the "comte" possessed.

I raised it so I could read it in the lamp light.

It was partly printed and partly handwritten. Goose bumps raced over my skin. That was the type of paper the maids had been searching for. The stock certificate was in Eleanor Neale's name. Worth 1,000 pounds! I lowered the paper. That was a large sum of money, though nothing like the fortune the comte held. If I remembered what Julian told me of stocks, owning this many shares not only gave one a portion of the profits but also a say in the company. How did Eleanor have this, and why? To someone, this might be worth killing for. But who knew about it? No one I'd spoken to gave any hint of it. Richard certainly hadn't.

But someone knew. Someone who had threatened the maids. Someone who had broken into the house to search the library.

My hands trembled. I had to put this somewhere safe. Somewhere safer. I needed to tell Richard—as soon as he woke. I needed more information.

What about Captain Reeves? He had been part of the East India Company. He might be able to tell me about Eleanor's connection to it, but he hadn't mentioned it before, even when I asked. Did he not know, or did he know too much?

I rushed out to find Julian.

He had settled himself in the drawing room with the chess board.

"Athena!" He stood. "Has Lord Neale—"

"He's still resting. I need to understand more about this." I held the paper out to him.

He took it, his eyebrows rising as he read. "That's a bold investment for a young lady. I suppose they belong to her brother now."

"If someone stole it, could they use it?"

He pursed his lips. "Well, they might be able to forge something giving them permission to sell her stocks, and then pocket the money."

"But this would give them a say in the company, too, wouldn't it?"

"Not anymore. Several years ago, the East India

Company raised the requirement to 2,000 pounds in stock to have a vote in the company's General Court. This is worth a great deal of money, but it doesn't offer any other advantages. Did you just find this?"

"I was going through Eleanor's papers and discovered it. I don't think even my husband knows about it. But I wonder if someone else might have. Someone dangerous."

"You think this has to do with her death?" Julian asked, looking at the paper again. "One thousand pounds is a great deal of money, but it still seems a small sum for such a terrible act."

I sighed and took the paper back. "You may be right. I wish I could find answers for her. And for Richard."

"Of course you do. Answers are comforting. When I think back to our time with Father, though, I realize that sometimes it's comforting enough just to have someone there in your troubles."

"Thank you again, brother. You are becoming a font of wisdom."

"I hope not! I'm not ready for that kind of responsibility."

I kissed him on the cheek and returned to Richard's chamber, dismissing Walters and taking up my vigil.

"I will be with you in your troubles," I whispered to Richard. "As long as you will let me."

He shifted, his brow creased in pain. I soothed it with a cool cloth.

I kept the stock certificate beside me throughout my vigil, my mind returning to it like a mill wheel circling again and again. I was still certain this was the paper the wolf wanted. But why?

Dawn had lightened the room when Richard stirred again. This time, his eyes looked tired but clear.

"Athena," he rasped.

"Richard. I am here." I felt his forehead and his cheek. Only a little warm. A burden melted from my chest, and I smiled. "You seem to be recovering."

He held my hand there against the side of his face for a moment. "The world won't be rid of me that easily."

"I am glad," I said softly.

He gave me a curious look. "Are you?"

"Yes." I found myself staring into his dark eyes, finally clear of the fever. Then I flushed and looked down.

My gaze fell on the stock certificate, and I thought of all I had done while Richard healed. I wanted to tell him every detail, but that might be too much until he regained his strength. Yet I did not want him agonizing over the comte.

I cleared my throat. "I ought to tell you something."

"Oh?" He sounded more drowsy than concerned.

"I discovered the comte's secret. He is no comte at all, but the eldest Reeves brother who made himself a new life in France. The Reeves must dance to the tune he asks them to play if they wish to keep their position."

"You discovered all that? How long have I been ill?" he asked.

I chuckled. "About a week. But the hints were there. I confronted him with the secret—"

Richard tensed.

"—and he doesn't care," I added quickly. "His ego is such that he fancies himself equally as important as a comte or a squire. I believe Eleanor suspected him, but I'm convinced he didn't harm her."

Richard sank back against his pillow, all color drained from his face. I had wanted to calm his mind, but I had distressed him instead. I pushed the stock certificate aside.

"What's that?" Richard asked.

I hesitated.

He grabbed my hand. "Tell me, what else did you find?"

"It can wait until you're well..."

"I'm well enough now if it's about Eleanor."

Unless I intended to flee the room with the paper, I was trapped.

I handed him the stock certificate. "I found this."

He looked confused for a moment, then he sighed. "Oh, Eleanor."

"You didn't know she had this?"

"No. After Father died, she had asked if she could invest a portion of her inheritance. I assumed she was buying stock in a bank like ladies in town sometimes do." He frowned for a long moment at the paper, and then he raised his eyebrows. "The roses!"

I looked at him. "Roses? Oh! They were coming from the Far East."

"Yes. She invested in the East Indies Company to have access to their botanists."

"And their roses," I said softly. "I suspect this is what the intruder was looking for. But it doesn't make sense. It's a large sum, but not worth...worth hurting someone."

His forehead creased.

I pressed on. "I wondered if someone wanted the control

it would give them in the company, but my brother tells me it's not enough."

"Not by itself." He trailed off, looking thoughtful.

My eyes widened. "If someone already had some shares, but not enough, they might want more. And if they knew that Eleanor had them… But why not just buy them from her? Surely, she didn't need them anymore once she had her roses."

"Maybe she still wanted them for sentimental reasons. Or maybe the person couldn't afford to pay." Something flashed in his eyes. "I must think on this." His expression softened. "You are tired. Let's both get some rest."

I agreed, but I left slowly, and I took the stock certificate with me. Richard was lying. He suspected who the killer was, and he was planning something. Well, he wasn't fit to ride out at the moment, and in the meantime, I could make plans, too.

CHAPTER 30

I collapsed into a deep sleep for several hours, waking to the afternoon sun. I wanted to peek in on Richard, but Walters stood guard over his sleep, assuring me his fever was still gone and his rest was a healing one.

Jane met me in the corridor. "How is he, my lady?"

I smiled. "Past the worst of it, I believe."

"I'm glad to hear it. Captain Reeves will be happy, too. He has been waiting downstairs, hoping for information."

"The captain is here?"

I thought of the East India Company shares with a shiver. But he would not have hurt Eleanor over money. It was time to see his reaction to the stock certificate.

"I had better speak to him," I told Jane.

I found Captain Reeves in the drawing room, reading one of the novels I had left there. He stood when I entered, his eyes worried.

"Captain," I said, sitting and motioning for him to do the

same. "Thank you for coming. You'll be glad to know you don't have to flee the country any time soon. Richard appears to be out of danger."

He smiled, lifting some of the weariness in his eyes. "I'm glad to hear it—as much for yours and Eleanor's sake as my own. But you still look concerned."

"I have discovered something I am trying to understand. Did you know that Eleanor owned stock in the East India Company? One thousand pounds worth, in fact."

His surprise seemed genuine. "I didn't. She had asked me about the company, and I told her my opinion of it."

"Which was?"

He sighed. "I have seen the damage it does. They are dealing in opium—addicting people to the drug and ruining many lives so they can have more control. Power. Money. She seemed as disgusted by it as I am." His forehead wrinkled. "I wonder why she would still buy stock in the company after that."

"I think she'd had the stock for some time. She bought it because it put her in contact with suppliers for the roses she could acquire from the East." I tapped my finger on the arm of my chair. "But why would she not sell the stock when she became disgusted by the company's actions? From what I know of her, she was principled."

"She was! She might have hoped to have a voice in changing the company, but at 1,000 pounds worth of shares, she no longer had a vote."

"Would she have before, as a woman?"

He shrugged. "Technically, yes, though they probably would have expected her to vote by a proxy."

"A thing she never did, since her brother likely would have known, and he was unaware of her shares."

"How did she buy them, then?" Captain Reeves asked. "Young ladies don't often walk into the Exchange to do business."

I cocked my head. "That's an excellent question. Who else did she know who had shares in the company? Or could have purchased them for her?"

The comte would not have bothered helping Eleanor. Besides, using his shares would have revealed his identity as Hugh Reeves, and 1,000 pounds was very little to him, who could already have a say in the company if he wished. There must be someone else who wanted her shares to add to his own.

He looked thoughtful. "The Reeves emphatically do not. Probably in protest against my father's interest in India."

"The comte does," I said, "But I don't think he knew or cared about Eleanor's."

Captain Reeves raised his eyebrows but didn't question me. I wondered if he knew or suspected the comte's true identity. If so, he gave nothing away.

"Who does that leave?" I asked. "Did Eleanor have many friends in London?"

"None I can imagine helping her secretly buy stocks. It likely would have been an older woman or a man. Maybe some friend of her father's."

My spine straightened with a jolt, and I felt ill. "The Palmers. They are old friends of the family."

His eyes widened. "Yes, it's possible. I have heard Mr.

Palmer speak of the Exchange. In fact, I had the sense that he was scrambling for new ways to make both ends meet.”

“Yes, he spoke about stock certificates at the Reeves’ dinner party. Could Mr. Palmer have hurt Eleanor, though? He seems so respectable.” Yet, I had been sure Mrs. Palmer was hiding something about the night of the party.

“He presents himself as a gentleman,” Captain Reeves said grimly. “But wolves often wear the guise of sheep.”

The Palmers struggled to maintain appearances while people like Mary Reeves snickered at their economy. Yet they did try to present a genteel image, attending parties like Eleanor’s. Visiting Bath. Mrs. Palmer had been in town when the murderer struck in the garden. Had her husband been there as well?

I stood, my knees trembly. “I need to ask Richard what he thinks of this idea.”

The captain nodded, his jaw set. “Please send word if you need any further help from me. I would like to see justice for Eleanor.”

I muttered my thanks and dashed back upstairs.

Walters still stood guard over Richard’s room.

“I need to see if Richard’s awake,” I told him.

He shifted. “He asked me to be sure no one disturbed his rest.”

Suspicion stirred in my chest. “Are you certain he’s in there?”

Walters opened his mouth, then shut it again. His raised his eyebrows at me and swung the door open.

Richard’s bed was empty.

CHAPTER 31

Walters and I stared in silent shock at the bed where, until so recently, Richard had fought for his life. A draft poured an icy chill through the room.

"Is there a servant's door?" I asked.

"Yes," Walters said grimly. "And that's how our fox slipped his den. But why?"

I pressed a hand against my churning stomach. "I have a suspicion. Where does he keep his pistols?"

Walters looked confused, but he checked a box on the dressing table. His face paled. "They're gone, my lady."

Cold gripped me. "He has taken them to confront Eleanor's killer."

"Do you know who it is, then?"

"I have a guess." I clasped my hands. "We have to hurry, though. What is he thinking? He's not fit to fight anyone."

Walters gave me a serious look. "That won't stop him. He's had a devil-may-care attitude since she died."

I straightened. If Richard would not be practical, I could. "Get horses. You are fetching Captain Reeves, and I am riding to the Palmers."

He nodded and raced from the room.

Jane hovered in the corridor. "Should I send for the constable as well?"

"I think you'd better not. We can hope this ends peacefully. But if something happens and we're not back soon, you'll know where to have them look."

Jane looked stricken by that thought, but she pressed her lips together and nodded.

I hurried after Walters to the stables. He helped me mount a placid-looking mare. I might have wished for a more dashing animal, but it had been years since I last rode, and breaking my neck would not help Richard. I managed a canter to the Palmer's house, my heart thudding a faster rhythm than the mare's hooves.

The old Tudor estate emerged from the trees. All seemed peaceful. I let out a tense breath. Maybe I had been wrong. Maybe Richard only needed some fresh air.

But as I slowed the mare, I spied Mrs. Palmer pacing in front of the house, wringing her hands. My stomach knotted. She turned at the sound my approach. Tears glistened on her cheeks.

She rushed to meet me.

"I'm so sorry," she gasped. "I hoped my suspicions were wrong. He acted so surly after Miss Neale's death, but I didn't want to believe—"

I slid from the mare. My legs trembled when they hit the ground. "Where are they?"

"Lord Neale chased him through the house with his pistol. They're going to kill each other!"

I hurried past her, entering the house cautiously. I had no weapon, and I didn't want to stumble into the midst of their fight. But I heard no shouting or thudding. Cold ran up my spine. Had Mr. Palmer overpowered Richard? Had Richard killed Mr. Palmer? That would not be the ending Eleanor wanted. My stomach twisted, and I grasped the banister. Not the ending I wanted. I longed to look into Richard's eyes again, to see his highwayman's smile, to feel his arms around me.

A voice—a plea—came from upstairs. My breath caught. I tiptoed up the stairs.

"If my arm were healed, I would strangle you like you did to her." Richard's hard words hit me like a blow. "Did she beg for mercy, or did you not give her the chance?"

A whimper led me to the open door of a bedchamber. Richard stood over a smashed jewelry box, the contents scattered over the floor. In the hand of his injured arm, he clutched a garnet bracelet. In the other, he held a pistol aimed at Mr. Palmer's chest. My throat tightened at the cold anger in his eyes.

"I would have given you the money," Richard said. "It's senseless!"

"It wasn't just the money." Mr. Palmer held his hands up, pleading. "I didn't have the shares to vote anymore when they raised the requirement to 2,000, and the blasted comte wouldn't part with any of his shares, though he bragged of holding them. I was only trying to regain my position. My respectability. But your sister had these stubborn ideas about the morality of the company. I didn't intend… I grew so frustrated when she kept saying no…"

Richard snarled, and his finger moved for the trigger.

"Richard! Don't!" I lunged forward to grab his arm.

Richard flashed a quick glance at me. "He murdered my sister. He murdered her for money and a stake in a filthy business."

"Yes," I said, trying to keep my voice steady as I glared at the cowering man. "He is worse than a wolf."

"It's my duty to avenge her."

I placed a hand on Richard's chest, my palm over the pounding of his heart. "Avenge her by seeing him off to prison. No doubt he will be hanged. But Eleanor would not want him to die at your hand. That's not the brother she admired." I glanced down at Palmer, who quivered before Richard's pistol. "He's not worth throwing everything away for. That isn't the story Eleanor wanted for you." I met Richard's eyes, pleading. "It's not the story I want for you."

We stood frozen in that terrible scene, Richard's pistol leveled at Palmer's chest. Palmer glanced between him and me, his eyes wide with terror.

"What story do you want for yourself?" I whispered.

Richard slowly lowered his pistol. Palmer sagged in relief. Richard stepped forward and smacked him in the temple with the butt of the pistol, sending Palmer unconscious to the ground.

"Eleanor will have justice," Richard growled. His shoulders relaxed, and the coldness left his eyes. "And we will have peace at Briarwood once again."

I wrapped my arms around him. "She would be proud of you."

He returned the embrace with his uninjured arm, burying his face against my neck. It felt so natural, like we belonged that way.

"She would have you to thank for it," he whispered. "We both do."

I melted into him. My eyes brimmed with tears of relief and joy. We had taken back our stories.

CHAPTER 32

I carried an armful of holly into the house, careful of the shiny, prickly leaves. Mr. Palmer was in gaol awaiting his trial, and Mrs. Palmer had been taken in by a widowed cousin who could offer her sympathy and companionship. The "comte" had announced he grew tired of the neighborhood and was taking his daughter to London, much to Ghislaine's relief. I didn't know if his exit was because I'd discovered his identity or because he was no longer the center of attention, but I was happy that Ghislaine was saved from an undesired marriage. And amid the new firestorm of gossip, Richard had consented to a restrained celebration of Christmastide.

I hung the holly so the carved faces of the entrance hall pillars peeked out like jolly children. Richard came up behind me as I worked. I didn't have to turn to know it was him—I was always aware when he was in the room. My fingers turned clumsy under his gaze, but when I glanced at him, he smiled.

"Eleanor would be pleased to see what you have done here," he said quietly.

I watched his face soften as he took in the display. Briarwood had been wrapped in a different kind of mourning over the last week as the truth of Eleanor's death reverberated around the countryside. Richard had observed it with grim satisfaction—not just at his name being cleared, but at the truth being made known and Eleanor finally receiving justice.

It left many questions hanging between us, and we had not found the space to discuss them with the constable and curious neighbors constantly dropping in, and Frances working to insinuate herself into as much of the action as possible.

Richard turned toward the ballroom, which I had left undecorated, and sorrow returned to his eyes. "It will be some time before Briarwood holds another ball."

"Of course." Answers did not erase the pain, but maybe they allowed for healing.

Richard pivoted to face me. "It pleases me as well. Seeing life return to Briarwood."

I looked down at the patterned rug. "I'm glad to know I've been of some service here."

He huffed out a laugh. "*Some* service? Athena, you saved Briarwood. You saved me."

I flushed and studied the sprig of holly in my hand.

"I lied to you," he blurted out. "About the party. With the garden. I did want to 'look you over.'"

I stared, trying to make sense of what he was saying.

"That's not quite right." He chuckled. "I had already 'looked you over' when I held up your brother's carriage. I liked what I saw. I wanted to be formally introduced. But the murder in the garden reminded me why that was a dangerous idea."

"Oh!" My face felt as warm as a yule log.

"And I came to believe that I had nothing to offer you. Perhaps not even safety. But now that you are safe, I will still offer you anything in my power. You can stay here as Lady Neale. If you don't want to stay at Briarwood, I will establish you in a house in London or wherever you desire. Or...or I will set you free, if it is what you wish."

My pulse hammered in my chest. I set the holly aside blindly, all my attention fixed on him.

"Richard," I said softly.

His eyes came to mine, hopeful and vulnerable. No masks.

My mouth went dry, and I fumbled for words. "You have already given me so much. You gave me the chance to see myself anew. To change my story. I was afraid to stay here, though, because there was one thing I wanted that I wasn't certain you could give me." I placed a hand on his chest. "Your heart."

"It has been broken," he whispered, "and it is still healing. But it is yours."

Warmth flowed through me, and a grin spread across my face for the first time in many days.

"Ahem," Jane said behind us.

We turned to see her hanging a sprig of mistletoe over

the entrance to the ballroom. She curtseyed, flashed a dimpled grin, and disappeared down the corridor.

Richard turned his mischievous highwayman's smile on me. "I never showed you the other thing we can do at Briarwood that we cannot do at Almack's."

"I think I would like to know about it," I said, my voice breathy.

He took me in his arms and waltzed me over to the ballroom entrance, a dizzy, floating dance that ended beneath the mistletoe. We stared at each other, my heart light and fluttering wildly.

Richard slowly pulled me closer and traced his fingers down my cheek. I closed my eyes and raised my face to his. His lips found mine, soft at first, and then more determined. I returned each kiss, forgetting everything in the world but the awareness of Richard.

"What is this!"

Frances's voice popped our bubble of bliss.

I opened my eyes to find Richard staring down at me, his eyes smiling.

"Really!" Frances said, storming down the corridor. "Such public displays are unseemly. I had hoped your scandalous behavior would come to an end, but if you carry on like this, people will say…say…"

"That I love my beautiful wife?" Richard asked, keeping his gaze on me.

I thought I might melt in his arms. He loved me. He thought me beautiful. Everything I had never dreamed possible.

"I love you, too," I whispered back.

Frances gasped like a fish tossed on the shore.

"Frances," Julian said from behind her. "It's their home. Leave them in peace and perhaps they will keep the mistletoe there for us to visit later."

Frances's face turned as red as the holly berries strung about the corridors. "Julian, what has come over you?"

"I realized that I don't have to live in the shadow of my father's mistakes—or anyone else's talk of scandal. I choose to face the sunlight instead." He took her hand and winked at me before leading her away.

I would swear I saw flashes of light twinkling like laughter from the holly boughs, but then Richard turned his full attention back to me.

"Now," he asked, his voice husky, "What were we discussing?"

"Things we cannot do at Almack's," I said with a giggle.

"Ah, yes. There are so many."

I grinned and leaned in to continue our "conversation." We still had many stories to tell.

Also by E.B. Wheeler

British Fiction:

Born to Treason

The Royalist's Daughter

The Haunting of Springett Hall

Wishwood (Westwood Gothic)

Moon Hollow (Westwood Gothic)

A Proper Dragon (Dragons of Mayfair 1)

An Elusive Dragon (Dragons of Mayfair 2)

A Subtle Dragon (Dragons of Mayfair 3)

Cruel Magic (Iron & Thorns 1)

Wild Magic (Iron & Thorns 2)

Fierce Magic (Iron & Thorns 3)

A Haunted Masquerade (A Haunted Season)

Utah Fiction:

No Peace with the Dawn (with Jeffery Bateman)

Letters from the Homefront (Utah at War)

Balm for the Heart (Utah at War)

Bootleggers and Basil (in *The Pathways to the Heart*)

Blood in a Dry Town (Tenny Mateo Mystery 1)

A Company of Bones (Tenny Mateo Mystery 2)

Nonfiction:

Utah Women: Pioneers, Poets & Politicians

Mysteries of the Old West

Mysteries of the Middle Ages

Mysteries of the Modern World

Juvenile Fiction:

The Bone Map

Alejandra the Axolotl and the Big Mess

Acknowledgments

Thanks for reading my novel. I hope you enjoyed it. I could not bring this book to publication without the support of a lot of people. Thank you to my critique group, The Writers' Cache, and to my beta readers Dan, Karen, Lauren, and Sharolyn for their insights. And as always, thank you to my family and to my husband for his unfailing support.

About the Author

E.B. Wheeler is the author of over a dozen books of history, historical fiction, and historical fantasy, including Whitney Award finalists *Born to Treason* and *A Proper Dragon,* and YA Fantasy Whitney Award winner *Cruel Magic*, as well as short stories, magazine articles, and scripts for educational software programs. She has a B.A. in history with an English minor from BYU and graduate degrees in history and landscape architecture from Utah State University. In addition to writing, she sometimes consults about historic preservation and teaches history, and she loves gardening, folk music, reading, and exploring the West with her husband and kids.